LITTLE MYTH MARKER

by

ROBERT ASPRIN

LITTLE MYTH MARKER

by ROBERT ASPRIN

**The Donning Company/
Publishers**
Norfolk/Virginia Beach

Starblaze Editions

Edited by Kay Reynolds

Other titles in this series:
Another Fine Myth
Myth Conceptions
Myth Directions
Hit or Myth
Myth-Ing Persons
Graphic novels:
Myth Adventures One
by Robert Asprin and Phil Foglio

Little Myth Marker is one of the many fantasy and science fiction titles published by The Donning Company/Publishers. For a complete listing of our titles, please write to the address below.

Copyright © 1985 by Robert L. Asprin

For information, write:
The Donning Company/Publishers
5659 Virginia Beach Boulevard
Norfolk, Virginia 23502

10 9 8 7 6 5 4 3 2 1

Library of Congress Cataloging-in-Publication Data:

Asprin, Robert.
   Little myth marker.
   I. Reynolds, Kay, 1951- . II. Title.
PS3551.S6L5   1985   813'.54   85-16296
ISBN 0-89865-411-4
ISBN 0-89865-418-1 (lim. ed.)
ISBN 0-89865-413-0 (pbk)

Cover and illustration copyright © 1985 Phil Foglio

Printed in the United States of America

Books by Robert Asprin
The Cold Cash War
The Bug Wars
Tambu
Mirror Friend, Mirror Foe (with George Takei)

The Myth Adventure Series:
Another Fine Myth
Myth Conceptions
Myth Directions
Hit or Myth
Myth-Ing Persons
Little Myth Marker

The Thieves' World Series (editor/author):
Thieves' World
Tales From the Vulgar Unicorn
Shadows of Sanctuary
Storm Season
Face of Chaos (with Lynn Abbey)
Wings of Omen (with Lynn Abbey)
Dead of Winter (with Lynn Abbey)

Graphic Novels:
Myth Adventures One (with Phil Foglio)
Myth Adventures Two (with Phil Foglio)
Thieves' World Graphics 1 (with Lynn Abbey)

Chapter I

*"The difference between an inside
straight and a blamed fool is callin'
the last bet!"*

B. Maverick

"Call!"
"Bump."
"Bump again."
"Who're you trying to kid? You got elf-high nothing!"
"Try me!"
"All right! Raise you limit."
"Call."
"Call."
"Elf-high nothing bumps you back limit."
"Fold."
"Call."
For those of you starting this book at the beginning
(Bless you! I hate it when readers cheat by reading

ahead!), this may be a little confusing. The above is the dialogue during a game of dragon poker. What is dragon poker, you ask? Well, it's reputed to be the most complicated card game ever invented...and here at the Bazaar at Deva, they should know.

The Bazaar is the biggest shopping maze and haggling spot in all the dimensions, and consequently gets a lot of dimension travelers (demons) passing through. In addition to the shops, stalls, and restaurants (which really doesn't do justice to the extent or variety of the Bazaar) there is a thriving gambling community in residence here. They are always on the lookout for a new game, particularly one that involves betting, and the more complicated the better. The basic philosophy is that a complicated game is more easily won by those who devote full time to its study than by the tourists who have dabbled in it or are trying to learn it as the game goes on. Anyway, when a Deveel bookie tells me that dragon poker is the most complicated card game ever, I tend to believe him.

"Fold."

"Call."

"Okay, Mr. Skeeve the Grater. Let's see you beat this! Dragons full!"

He exposed his hole cards with a flourish that bordered on a challenge. Actually, I had been hoping he would drop out of the hand. This particular individual (Grunk, I think his name was) was easily two heads taller than me and had bright red eyes, canines almost as long as my forearm, and a nasty disposition. He tended to speak in an angry shout, and the fact that he had been losing steadily had not mellowed him in the slightest.

"Well? C'mon! What have you got?"

I turned over my four hole cards, spread them next to the five already face up, then leaned back and smiled.

"That's it?" Grunk said, craning his neck and scowling at my cards. "But that's only...."

2

"Wait a minute," the player on his left chimed in. "It's Tuesday. That makes his unicorns wild."

"But it's a month with an 'M' in it!" someone else piped up. "So his ogre is only half of face value!"

"But there's an even number of players...."

I told you it was a complicated game. Those of you who know me from my earlier adventures (blatant plug!) may wonder how it is I understand such a complex system. That's easy. I don't! I just bet, then spread the cards and let the other players sort out who won.

You may wonder what I was doing sitting in on a cutthroat game of dragon poker when I didn't even know the rules. Well, for once, I have an answer. I was enjoying myself on my own for a change.

You see, ever since Don Bruce, the Mob's fairy godfather, supposedly hired me to watch over the Mob's interests at the Bazaar and assigned me two bodyguards, Guido and Nunzio, I've rarely had a moment to myself. This weekend, however, my two watchdogs were off making their yearly report to Mob Central, leaving me to fend for myself. Obviously, before they left, they made me give my solemn promise to be careful. Also obviously, as soon as they were gone, I set out to do just the opposite.

Even aside from our percentage of the Mob's take at the Bazaar, our magic business had been booming, so money was no problem. I filched a couple thousand in gold from petty cash and was all set to go on a spree when an invitation arrived to sit in on one of the Geek's dragon poker games at his club, the Even-Odds.

As I said before, I know absolutely nothing about dragon poker other than the fact that at the end of a hand you have five cards face up and four face down. Anytime I've tried to get my partner, Aahz, to teach me more about the game, I've been lectured about "only playing games you know" and "don't go looking for trouble." Since I was already looking for mischief, the chance to

3

defy both my bodyguards *and* my partner was too much to resist. I mean, I figured the worst that could happen was that I'd lose a couple thousand in gold. Right?

"You're all overlooking something. This is the forty-third hand and Skeeve there is sitting in a chair facing north!"

I took my cue from the groans and better-censored expressions of disgust and raked in the pot.

"Say, Geek," Grunk said, his red eyes glittering at me through half-lowered eyelids. "Are you *sure* this Skeeve fellow isn't using magic?"

"Guaranteed," responded the Deveel who was gathering the cards and shuffling for the next hand. "Any game I host here at the Even-Odds is monitored against magic *and* telepathy."

"Weelll, I don't normally play cards with magicians, and I've heard that Skeeve here is supposed to be pretty good in that department. Maybe he's good enough that you just can't catch him at it."

I was starting to get a little nervous. I mean, I wasn't using magic...and even if I was going to, I wouldn't know how to use it to rig a card game. The trouble was that Grunk looked perfectly capable of tearing my arms off if he thought I was cheating. I began racking my brain for some way to convince him without admitting to everyone at the table just how little I knew about magic.

"Relax, Grunk. Mr. Skeeve's a good player, that's all. Just because he wins doesn't mean he's cheating."

That was Pidge, the only other human-type in the game. I shot him a grateful smile.

"I don't mind someone winning," Grunk muttered defensively, "But he's been winning all night."

"I've lost more than you have," Pidge said, "and you don't see me griping. I'm tellin' you Mr. Skeeve is *good*. I've sat in on games with the Kid, and I should know."

"The Kid? You've played against him?" Grunk was

4

visibly impressed.

"And lost my socks doing it," Pidge admitted wryly. "I'd say that Mr. Skeeve here is good enough to give him a run for his money, though."

"Gentlemen? Are we here to talk or to play cards?" the Geek interrupted, tapping the deck meaningfully.

"I'm out," Pidge said, rising to his feet. "I know when I'm outclassed—even if I have to go in the hole before I'll admit it. My marker still good, Geek?"

"It's good with me if nobody else objects."

Grunk noisily slammed his fist down on the table, causing several of my stacks of chips to fall over.

"What's this about markers?" he demanded. "I thought this was a cash-only game! Nobody said anything about playing for IOUs."

"Pidge here's an exception," the Geek said. "He's always made good on his marker before. Besides, you don't have to worry about it, Grunk. You aren't even getting all of *your* money back."

"Yeah. But I lost it betting against somebody who's betting markers instead of cash. It seems to me . . ."

"I'll cover his marker," I said loftily. "That makes it personal between him and me, so it doesn't involve anyone else at the table. Right, Geek?"

"That's right. Now shut up and play, Grunk. Or do you want us to deal you out?"

The monster grumbled a bit under his breath but leaned back and tossed in another chip to ante for the next hand.

"Thanks, Mr. Skeeve," Pidge said. "And don't worry. Like the Geek says, I always reclaim my marker."

I winked at him and waved vaguely as he left, already intent on the next hand as I tried vainly to figure out the rules of the game.

If my grand gesture seemed a little impulsive, remember that I'd been watching him play all night, and I knew how much he had lost. Even if all of it was on

IOUs, I could cover it out of my winnings and still show a profit.

You see, Grunk was right. I had been winning steadily all night...a fact made doubly surprising by my ignorance of the game. Early on, however, I had hit on a system which seemed to be working very well: Bet the players, not the cards. On the last hand, I hadn't been betting that I had a winning hand, I was betting that Grunk had a losing hand. Luck had been against him all night, and he was betting wild to try to make up for his losses.

Following my system, I folded the next two hands, then hit them hard on the third. Most of the other players folded rather than question my judgment. Grunk stayed until the bitter end, hoping I was bluffing. It turned out that I was (my hand wasn't all that strong), but that his hand was even weaker. Another stack of chips tumbled into my hoard.

"That does it for me," Grunk said, pushing his remaining chips toward the Geek. "Cash me in."

"Me too."

"I should have left an hour ago. Would have saved myself a couple hundred."

The Geek was suddenly busy converting chips back to cash as the game broke up.

Grunk loitered for a few minutes after receiving his share of the bank. Now that we were no longer facing each other over cards, he was surprisingly pleasant.

"You know, Skeeve," he said, clapping a massive hand on my shoulder, "it's been a long time since I've been whipped that bad at dragon poker. Maybe Pidge was right. You're slumming here. You should try for a game with the Kid."

"I was just lucky."

"No. I'm serious. If I knew how to get in touch with him, I'd set up the game myself."

"You won't have to," one of the other players put in

as he started for the door. "Once word of this game gets around, the Kid will come looking for you."

"True enough," Grunk laughed over his shoulder. "Really, Skeeve. If that match-up happens, be sure to pass the word to me. That's a game I'd like to see."

"Sure, Grunk," I said. "You'll be one of the first to know. Catch you later."

Actually, my mind was racing as I made my goodbyes. This was getting out of hand. I had figured on one madcap night on my own, then calling it quits without anyone else the wiser. If the other players started shooting their mouths off all over the Bazaar, there would be no hope of keeping my evening's adventure a secret...particularly from Aahz! The only thing that would be worse would be if I ended up with some hot-shot gambler hunting me down for a challenge match.

"Say, Geek," I said, trying to make it sound casual. "Who is this 'Kid' they keep talking about?"

The Deveel almost lost his grip on the stack of chips he was counting. He gave me a long stare, then shrugged.

"You know, Skeeve, sometimes I don't know when you're kidding me and when you're serious. I keep forgetting that as successful as you are, you're still new to the Bazaar...and to gambling specifically."

"Terrific. Who's the 'Kid'?"

"The Kid's the current king of the dragon poker circuit. His trademark is that he always includes a breath mint with his opening bet for each hand...says that it brings him luck. That's why they call him the 'Sen-Sen Ante Kid.' I'd advise you to stay away from him, though. You had a good run tonight, but the Kid is the best there is. He'd eat you alive in a head-to-head game."

"I hear that." I laughed. "I was only curious. Really. Just cash me in and I'll be on my way."

The Geek gestured at the stacks of coins on the table.

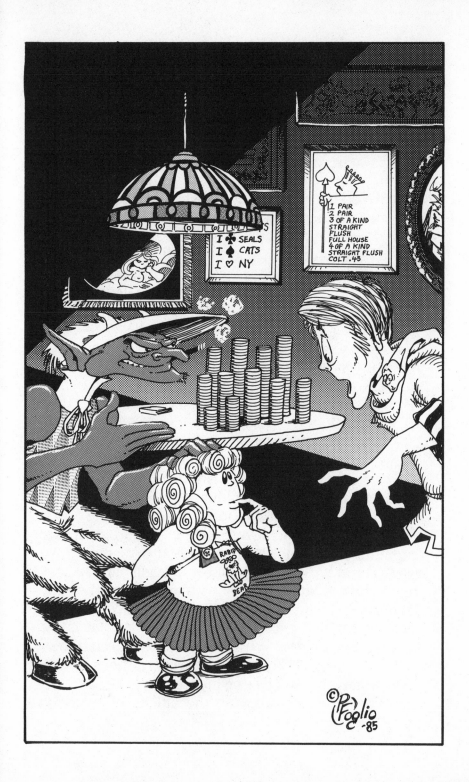

"What's to cash?" he said. "I pulled mine out the same time I cashed the others' out. The rest is yours."

I looked at the money and swallowed hard. For the first time I could understand why some people found gambling so addictive. There was easily twenty thousand in gold weighing down the table. All mine. From one night of cards!

"Um...Geek? Could you hold on to my winnings for me? I'm not wild about the idea of walking around with that much gold on me. I can drop back by later with my bodyguards to pick it up."

"Suit yourself," the Geek shrugged. "I can't think of anyone at the Bazaar who would have nerve enough to jump you, with your reputation. Still, you might run into a stranger...."

"Fine," I said, heading for the door. "Then I'll be..."

"Wait a minute! Aren't you forgetting something?"

"What's that?"

"Pidge's marker. Hang on and I'll get it."

He disappeared before I could protest, so I leaned against the wall to wait. I had forgotten about the marker, but the Geek was a gambler and adhered more religiously to the unwritten laws of gambling than most folks obeyed civil law. I'd just have to humor him and...

"Here's the marker, Skeeve," the Deveel announced. "Markie, this is Skeeve."

I just gaped at him, unable to speak. Actually, I gaped at the little blond-headed moppet he was leading by the hand. That's right. A girl. Nine or ten years old at the most.

I experienced an all-too-familiar sinking feeling in my stomach that meant I was in trouble...lots of it.

Chapter II

*"Kids? Who said anything
about kids?"*

Conan

THE LITTLE GIRL looked at me through eyes that glowed with trust and love. She barely stood taller than my waist and had that wholesome, healthy glow that young girls are all supposed to have but so few actually do. With her little beret and matching jumper, she looked so much like an oversized doll that I wondered if she'd say "Mama" if you turned her upside down, then right-side up again.

She was so adorable that it was obvious that anyone with a drop of paternal instinct would fall in love with her on sight. Fortunately, my partner had trained me well; any instincts I had were of a more monetary nature.

"What's that?" I demanded.

"It's a little girl," the Geek responded. "Haven't you

ever seen one before?"

For a minute, I thought I was being baited. Then I remembered some of my earliest conversations with Aahz and controlled my temper.

"I realize that it's a little girl, Geek," I said carefully. "What I was really trying to ask is a) who is she? b) what is she doing here? and c) what has this got to do with Pidge's marker? Do I make myself clear?"

The Deveel blinked his eyes in bewilderment.

"But I just told you. Her name is Markie. She's Pidge's marker...you know, the one you said you would cover personally?"

My stomach bottomed out.

"Geek, we were talking about a piece of paper. You know, 'IOU, etc.'? A marker! Who leaves a little girl for a marker?"

"Pidge does. Always has. C'mon, Skeeve. You know me. Would I give anyone credit for a piece of paper? I give Pidge credit on Markie here because I know he'll be back to reclaim her."

"Right. *You* give him credit. I don't deal in little girls, Geek."

"You do now," he smiled. "Everyone at the table heard you say so. I'll admit I was a little surprised at the time."

"...But not surprised enough to warn me about what I was buying into. Thanks a lot, Geek old pal. I'll try to remember to return the favor someday."

In case you didn't notice, that last part was an open threat. As has been noted, I've been getting quite a reputation around the Bazaar as a magician, and I didn't really think the Geek wanted to be on my bad side.

Okay. So it was a rotten trick. I was getting desperate.

"Whoa. Hold it," the Deveel said quickly. "No reason to get upset. If you don't want her, I'll give you cash to cover the marker and keep her myself..."

"That's better."

"...at the usual terms, of course."

I knew I was being suckered. *Knew* it, mind you. But I had to ask anyway.

"What terms?"

"If Pidge doesn't reclaim her in two weeks, I sell her into slavery for enough money to cover her father's losses."

Check and mate.

I looked at Markie. She was still holding the Geek's hand, listening solemnly while we argued out her fate. As our eyes met, she said her first words since she had entered the room.

"Are you going to be my new daddy?"

I swallowed hard.

"No, I'm not your daddy, Markie. I just..."

"Oh, I know. It's just that every time my *real* daddy leaves me with someone, he tells me that they're going to be my pretend daddy for a while. I'm supposed to mind them and do what they tell me just as if they were my real daddy until my real daddy comes to get me. I just wanted to know if you were going to be my new pretend daddy?"

"Ummm..."

"I hope so. You're nice. Not like some of the scumbags he's left me with. Will you be my new daddy?"

With that, she reached out and took hold of my hand. A small thrill ran through me like an autumn shiver. She was so vulnerable, so trusting. I had been on my own for a long time, first alone, then apprenticed to Garkin, and finally teamed with Aahz. In all that time, I had never really been responsible for another person. It was a funny feeling, scary and warming at the same time.

I tore my eyes away from her and glared at the Geek again.

"Slavery's outlawed here at the Bazaar."

The Deveel shrugged. "There are other dimensions. As a matter of fact, I've had a standing offer for her for several years. That's why I've been willing to accept her as collateral. I could make enough to cover the bet, the cost of the food she's eaten over the years, and still turn a tidy profit."

"That's about the lowest..."

"Hey! The name's 'the Geek,' not 'the Red Cross'! I don't do charity. Folks come to me to bet, not for handouts."

I haven't thrown a punch at anyone since I started practicing magic, but I was sorely tempted to break that record just this once. Instead, I turned to the little girl.

"Get your things, Markie. Daddy's taking you to your new home."

* * *

My partner and I were currently basing our operations at the Bazaar at Deva, which is the home dimension of the Deveels. Deveels are reputed to be the sharpest merchants, traders, and hagglers in all the known dimensions. You may have heard of them in various folk tales in your own home dimension. Their fame lingers even in dimensions they have long since stopped trading in.

The Bazaar is the showcase of Deva...in fact, I've never seen a part of Deva that wasn't the Bazaar. Here the Deveels meet to trade with each other, buying and selling the choicest magics and miracles from all the dimensions. It's an around-the-clock, over-the-horizon sprawl of tents, shops, and barter blankets where you can acquire anything your imagination can conjure as well as a lot of things you never dreamed existed...for a price. Many inventors and religious figures have built their entire career from items purchased in one trip to the Bazaar. Needless to say, it is devastating to the

13

average budget...even if the holder of the pursestrings has above-average sales resistance.

Normally I enjoy strolling through the booths, but tonight, with Markie beside me, I was too distracted to concentrate on the displays. It occurred to me that, fun as it is for adults, the Bazaar is no place to raise a child.

"Will we be living by ourselves, or do you have a girlfriend?"

Markie was clinging to my hand as we made our way through the Bazaar. The wonders of the stalls and shops dispensing magic reached out to us as they always do, but she was oblivious to them, choosing instead to ply me with questions and hanging on my every word.

"'No' to both questions. Tananda lives with me, but she isn't my girlfriend. She's a free-lance assassin who helps me out on jobs from time to time. Then there's Chumley, her brother. He's a troll who works under the name of Crunch. You'll like them. They're nice...in a lot of ways they're nicer than I am."

Markie bit her lip and frowned. "I hope you're right. I've found that a lot of nice people don't like little kids."

"Don't worry," I said, with more confidence than I felt. "But I'm not done yet. There's also Guido and Nunzio, my bodyguards. They may seem a little gruff, but don't let them scare you. They just act tough because it's part of their job."

"Gee. I've never had a daddy who had bodyguards before."

"That's not all. We also have Buttercup, who's a war unicorn, and Gleep, who's my very own pet dragon."

"Oh, lots of people have dragons. I'm more impressed by the bodyguards."

That took me aback a little. I'd always thought that having a dragon was rather unique. I mean, nobody else I knew had a dragon. Then again, nobody else I knew had bodyguards, either.

"Let's see," Markie was saying. "There's Tananda,

14

Chumley, Guido, Nunzio, Buttercup, and Gleep. Is that all?"

"Well, there's also Massha. She's my apprentice."

"Massha. That's a pretty name."

Now, there are lots of words to describe my apprentice, but unfortunately 'pretty' isn't one of them. Massha is huge, both in height and breadth. There are large people who still manage to look attractive, but my apprentice isn't one of them. She tends toward loud, colorful clothes which invariably clash with her bright orange hair, and wears enough jewelry for three stores. In fact, the last time she got into a fight here at the Bazaar was when a nearsighted shopper mistook her for a display tent.

"Aahh...you'll just have to meet her. But you're right. Massha is a pretty name."

"Gee, you've got a lot of people living with you."

"Well...umm...there *is* one more."

"Who's that?"

"His name is Aahz. He's my partner."

"Is he nice, too?"

I was torn between loyalty and honesty."

"He...aah...takes getting used to. Remember how I told you not to be scared of the bodyguards even if they were a little gruff?"

"Yes."

"Well, it's all right to be scared of Aahz. He gets a little upset from time to time, and until he cools down it's best to give him a lot of room and not leave anything breakable—like your arm—within his reach."

"What gets him upset?"

"Oh, the weather, losing money, not making money...which to him is the same as losing money, any one of a hundred things that I say...and you! I'm afraid he's going to be a little upset when he meets you, so stay behind me until I get him calmed down. Okay?"

"Why would he be upset with me?"

"You're going to be a surprise to him, and he doesn't like surprises. You see, he's a very suspicious person and tends to think of a surprise as a part of an unknown plot against him...or me."

Markie lapsed into silence. Her brow furrowed as she stared off into nothingness, and it occurred to me that I was scaring her.

"Hey, don't worry," I said, squeezing her hand. "Aahz will be okay once he gets over being surprised. Now tell me about yourself. Do you go to school?"

"Yes. I'm halfway through Elemental School. I'd be further if we didn't keep moving around."

"Don't you mean Elementary School?" I smiled.

"No. I mean..."

"Whoops. Here we are. This is your new home, Markie."

I gestured grandly at the small tent that was our combination home and headquarters.

"Isn't it a little small for all those people?" she frowned, staring at the tent.

"It's bigger inside than it is outside," I explained. "C'mon. I'll show you."

I raised the flap for her and immediately wished I hadn't.

"Wait'll I get my hands on him!" came Aahz's booming voice from within. "After all the times I've told him to stay away from dragon poker!"

It occurred to me that maybe we should wait for a while before introducing Markie to my partner. I started to ease the flap down, but it was too late.

"Is that you, partner? I'd like to have a little chat, if you don't mind!"

"Remember. Stay behind me," I whispered to Markie, then proceeded to walk into the lion's den.

Chapter III

"I'm doing this for your own good!"
any establishment executioner...
or any parent

AS I TOLD Markie, our place at the Bazaar was bigger on the inside than on the outside...lots bigger! I've been in smaller palaces...heck, I've lived and worked in smaller palaces than our current domicile. Back when I was court magician at Possletum, to be exact.

Here at the Bazaar, the Deveels think that any display of wealth will weaken their position when they haggle over prices, so they hide the size of their homes by tucking them into 'unlisted dimensions.' Even though our home looked like just a humble tent from the street, the inside included multiple bedrooms, a stable area, a courtyard and garden, etc., etc. You get the picture.

Unfortunately for me, at the moment it also included my partner, Aahz.

"Well, if it isn't the Bazaar's own answer to War, Famine, Death, and Pestilence! Other dimensions have the Four Horsemen, but the Bazaar at Deva has the Great Skeeve!"

Remember my partner, Aahz? I mentioned him back in Chapter One and again in Chapter Two. Most of my efforts to describe him fail to prepare people for the real thing. What I usually forget to mention to folks is that he's from the dimension Perv. For those of you unfamiliar with dimension travel, that means he is green and scaly with a mouth big enough for any other three beings and teeth enough for a school of sharks. . .if shark's teeth got to be four inches long, that it. I don't deliberately omit things from my descriptions. It's just that after all these years I've gotten used to him.

"Have you got anything at all to say for yourself? Not that there's any acceptable excuse, mind you. It's just that tradition allows you a few last words."

Well. . .I've *almost* gotten used to him.

"Hi, Aahz. Have you heard about the card game?"

"About two hours ago," Massha supplied from a nearby chair where she was entrenched with a book and a huge box of chocolates. "He's been like this ever since."

"I see you've done your usual marvelous job of calming him down."

"I'm just an apprentice around here," she said with a shrug. "Getting between you two in a quarrel is not part of my game plan for a long and prosperous life."

"If you two are *quite* through," Aahz growled, "I'm still waiting to hear what you have to say for yourself."

"What's to say? I sat in on a game of dragon poker. . . ."

"WHO'S BEEN TEACHING YOU TO PLAY DRAGON POKER? That's what there is to say! Was it Tananda? Chumley? How come you're going to other people for lessons all of a sudden? Aren't I good enough for the Great Skeeve any more?"

The truth of the situation suddenly dawned on me. Aahz was my teacher before he insisted that I be elevated to full partner status. Even though we were theoretically equals, old habits die hard and he still considered himself to be my exclusive teacher, mentor, coach, and all-around nudge. What the *real* problem was was that my partner was jealous of someone else horning in on what he felt was his private student! Perhaps this problem would be easier to deal with than I thought.

"No one else has been teaching me, Aahz. Everything I know about dragon poker, I learned from you."

"But I haven't taught you anything."

"Exactly."

That stopped him. At least, it halted his pacing as he turned to peer suspiciously at me with his yellow eyes.

"You mean you don't know anything at all about dragon poker?"

"Well, from listening to you talk, I know about how many cards are dealt out and stuff like that. I still haven't figured out what the various hands are, much less their order...you know, what beats what."

"*I* know," my partner said pointedly. "What I don't know is why you decided to sit in on a game you don't know the first thing about."

"The Geek sent me an invitation, and I thought it would be sociable to..."

"The Geek? You sat in at one of the Geek's games at the Even-Odds to be sociable?" He was off again. "Don't you know that those are some of the most cutthroat games at the Bazaar? They eat amateurs alive at those tables. And you went there to be sociable?"

"Sure. I figured the worse that could happen would be that I lost a little money. The way things have been going, we can afford it. Besides, who knows, I might get lucky."

"Lucky? Now I know you don't know anything

about dragon poker. It's a game of skill, not luck. All you could do was throw your money away...money we've both risked our lives for, I might add."

"Yes, Aahz."

"And besides, one of the first things you learn playing any kind of poker is that the surest way to lose is to go in *expecting* to lose."

"Yes, Aahz."

Out of desperation, I was retreating behind my strongest defense. I was agreeing with everything he said. Even Aahz has trouble staying mad at someone who's agreeing with him.

"Well, what's done is done and all the shouting in the world won't change it. I just hope you've learned your lesson. How much did it cost you, anyway?"

"I won."

"Okay. Just to show you there're no hard feelings, we'll split it. In a way it's my fault. I should have taught you..."

There was a sudden stillness in the room. Even Massha had stopped with a bonbon halfway to her mouth. Very slowly, Aahz turned to face me.

"You know, Skeeve, for a minute there, I thought you said..."

"I won," I repeated, trying desperately not to smile.

"You won. As in 'better than broke even' won?"

"As in 'twenty thousand in gold plus' won," I corrected.

"But if you didn't know how the game was played, how could you..."

"I just bet the people, not the cards. It seemed to work out pretty well."

I was in my glory now. It was a rare time indeed that I managed to impress my partner, and I was going to milk it for all it was worth.

"But that's crazy!" Aahz scowled. "I mean, it could work for a while, but in the long run..."

"He was great!" Markie announced, emerging from behind me. "You should have seen it. He beat everybody."

My "glory" came tumbling down around my ears. With one hand I shoved Markie back behind me and braced for the explosion. What I really wanted to do was run for cover, but that would have left Markie alone in the open, so I settled for closing my eyes.

Nothing happened.

After a few moments, I couldn't stand the suspense any more and opened one eye to sneak a peek. The view I was treated to was an *extreme* close-up of one of Aahz's yellow eyes. He was standing nose to nose with me, apparently waiting until I was ready before launching into his tirade. It was obvious that *he* was ready. The gold flecks in his eyes were shimmering as if they were about to boil...and for all I knew, they were.

"Who...is...that?"

I decided against trying to play dumb and say "Who is what?" At the range he was standing, Aahz would have bitten my head off...literally!

"Umm...remember I said that I won twenty thousand plus? Well, she's the plus."

"YOU WON A KID IN A CARD GAME!?!!"

The force of my partner's voice actually knocked me back two steps. I probably would have gone farther if I hadn't bumped against Markie.

"ARE YOU OUT OF YOUR MIND?? DON'T YOU KNOW THE PENALTY FOR SLAVERY IS..."

He disappeared in mid-sentence behind a wall of flesh and tasteless color. Despite her earlier claims of valuing self-preservation, Massha had stepped between us.

"Just cool down a minute, Green and Scaly."

Aahz tried to get around her.

"BUT HE JUST..."

She took a half step sideways and blocked him by leaning against the wall.

"Give him a chance to explain. He *is* your partner, isn't he?"

From the sound of his voice, Aahz reversed his field and tried for the other side.

"BUT HE . . ."

Massha took two steps and leaned against the other wall, all the while talking as if she wasn't being interrupted.

"Now either he's an idiot . . . which he isn't, or you're a lousy teacher . . . which you aren't, or there's more to this than meets the eye. Hmmm?"

There were several moments of silence, then Aahz spoke again in a voice much more subdued.

"All right, *partner.* Let's hear it."

Massha relinquished her spot and I could see Aahz again . . . though I almost wished I couldn't. He was breathing hard, but whether from anger or from the exertion of trying to get around Massha I couldn't tell. I could hear the scales on his fingers rasp as he clenched and unclenched his fists, and I knew that I'd better tell my story fast before he lost control again.

"I didn't win *her,*" I said hastily. "I won her father's marker. She's our guarantee that he'll come back and make his losses good."

Aahz stopped making with the fists, and a puzzled frown creased his features.

"A marker? I don't get it. The Geek's games are always on a cash-and-carry basis."

"Well, he seems to have made an exception in Pidge's case.

"Pidge?"

"That's my daddy," Markie announced, stepping from behind me again. It's short for Pigeon. He loses a lot . . . that's why everyone is always so happy to let him sit in on a game."

"Cute kid," Aahz said drily. "It also might explain why you did so well in the game tonight. One screwball

22

can change the pace of an entire game. Still, when the Geek *does* take markers, he usually pays the winners in cash and handles the collecting himself."

"He was willing to do that."

"Then why..."

"...and if Markie's father didn't show up in two weeks, he was going to take her off-dimension and sell her into slavery himself to raise the money."

From her chair, Massha gave a low whistle.

"Sweet guy, this Geek."

"He's a Deveel." Aahz waved absently, as if the statement explained everything. "Okay, okay. I can see where you felt you had to accept custody of the kid here instead of leaving her with the Geek. Just answer me one question."

"What's that?"

"What do *we* do with her if her father doesn't show up?"

Sometimes I like it better when Aahz is ranting than when he's thinking.

"Aahh...I'm still working on that one."

"Terrific. Well, when you come up with an answer, let me know. I think I'll stay in my room until this whole thing blows over."

With that he strode out of the room, leaving Massha and me to deal with Markie.

"Cheer up, Hot Stuff," my apprentice said. "Kids aren't all that much of a problem. Hey, Markie. Would you like a piece of chocolate?"

"No, thank you. It might make me fat and ugly like you."

I winced. Up until now, Massha had been my ally on the subject of Markie, but this might change everything. She was very sensitive about her weight, so most of us tended to avoid any mention of it. In fact, I had gotten so used to her appearance that I tended to forget how she looked to anyone who didn't know her.

"Markie!" I said sternly. "That wasn't a very nice

thing to say."

"But it's true!" she countered, turning her innocent eyes on me.

"That's why it's not nice," Massha laughed, though I noticed her smile was a little forced. "C'mon, Markie. Let's hit the pantry and try to find you something to eat...something low-calorie."

The two of them trooped out, leaving me alone with my thoughts. Aahz had raised a good question. What *were* we going to do if Markie's father didn't come back? I had never been around kids before. I knew that having her around would cause problems, but how many problems? With everything else we had handled as a team, surely Aahz and I could handle a little girl. Of course, Aahz was...

"There you are, Boss! Good. I was hopin' you were still up."

I cleared my mind to find one of my bodyguards entering the room.

"Oh. Hi, Guido. How did the report go?"

"Couldn't be better. In fact, Don Bruce was so happy he sent you a little present."

In spite of my worries, I couldn't help smiling. At least *something* was going right.

"That's great," I said. "I could use a little cheering up just now."

"Then I've got just the thing. Hey, Nunzio! Bring her in here!"

My smile froze. I tried desperately not to panic. After all, I reasoned, people refer to a lot of things as "her." Boats, for example, or even...

"Boss, this is Bunny. Don Bruce sends her with his compliments on a job well done. She's going to be your moll."

The girl they were escorting into the room bore no resemblance at all to a boat.

Chapter IV

"A doll is a doll is a doll."

F. Sinatra

BUNNY WAS a top-heavy little redhead with her hair in a pixie cut and a vacant stare a zombie would envy. She was vigorously chewing something as she rubbernecked, trying to take in the entire room at once.

"Gee. This is quite a place you guys's got here. It's a lot nicer than the last place I was at, ya know?"

"This is just the waitin' room," Nunzio said with pride. "Wait'll you see the rest of the layout. It's bigger'n any hangout I've ever worked, know what I mean?"

"What'sa matter with you two?" Guido barked. "Ain't ya got no manners? First things first. Bunny, this is the Boss. He's the one you're goin' to be workin' under."

Bunny advanced toward me holding out her hand. From the way her body moved under her tight-fitting clothes, there was little doubt what she was wearing

25

under them...or not wearing, as the case may be.

"Pleased ta meetcha, Boss. The pleasure's mutual," she said brightly.

For once, I knew exactly what to say.

"No."

She stopped, then turned toward Guido with a frown.

"He means not to call him 'Boss' until you get to know him," my bodyguard assured her. "Around here he's just known as Skeeve."

"Gotcha," she winked. "Okay, *Skeeve*...ya know, that's kinda cute."

"No," I repeated.

"Okay. So it's not cute. Whatever you say. You're the Boss."

"NO!"

"But..."

I ignored her and turned directly to Guido.

"Have you lost your marbles? What are you doing bringing her in here like this?"

"Like I said, Boss, she's a present from Don Bruce."

"Guido, lots of people give each other presents. Presents like neckties and books...not girls!"

My bodyguard shrugged his shoulders helplessly. "So Don Bruce ain't lots of people. He's the one who assigned us to you in the first place, and he says that someone with your standin' in the Mob should have a moll."

"Guido...let's talk. Excuse us a minute, Bunny."

I slipped an arm around my bodyguard's shoulders and drew him off into a corner. That may sound easy until you realize I had to reach *up* to get to his shoulders. Both Guido and Nunzio are considerably larger than me.

"Now look, Guido," I said. "Remember when I explained our setup to you?"

"Sure, Boss."

"Well, let's walk through it again. Don Bruce hired

26

Aahz and me on a non-exclusive basis to watch over the Mob's interests here at the Bazaar. Now, he did that because the ordinary methods he employs weren't working....Right?"

"Actually, he hired *you* and included your partner. Except for that...right."

"Whatever. We also explained to you that the reason the Mob's usual methods weren't working was that the Bazaar merchants had hired us to chase the Mob out. Remember?"

"Yea. That was really a surprise when you told us. You really had us goin', know what I mean?"

"Now that brings us to the present. The money we're collecting from the Bazaar merchants and passing on to Don Bruce, the money he thinks they're paying the Mob for protection, is actually being paid to us to keep the Mob away from the Bazaar. Get it?"

"Got it."

"Good. Then, understanding the situation as you do, you can see why I don't want a moll or anyone else from the Mob hanging around. If word gets back to Don Bruce that we're flim-flamming him, it'll reopen the whole kettle of worms. That's why you've got to get rid of her."

Guido nodded vigorously.

"No," he said.

"Then all you have to...what do you mean, 'no'? Do I have to explain it all to you again?"

My bodyguard heaved a great sigh.

"I understand the situation, Boss. But I don't think *you* do. Allow me to continue where you left off."

"But I..."

"Now, whatever you are, Don Bruce considers you to be a minor chieftain in the Mob running a profitable operation. Right?"

"Well..."

"As such, you are entitled to a nice house, which

you have, a couple of bodyguards, which you have, and a moll, which you don't have. These things are necessary in Don Bruce's eyes if the Mob is to maintain its public image of rewarding successful members...just as it finds it necessary to express its displeasure at members who fail. Follow me?"

"Public image," I said weakly.

"So it is in the interests of the Mob that Don Bruce has provided you with what you have failed to provide yourself...namely: a moll. If you do not like this one, we can take her back and get another, but a moll you must have if we are to continue in our existing carefree manner. Otherwise..." He paused dramatically.

"Otherwise...?" I prompted.

"If you do not maintain the appearance of a successful Mob member, Don Bruce will be forced to deal with you as if you were unsuccessful...know what I mean?"

I suddenly felt the need to massage my forehead. "Terrific."

"My sentiments exactly. Under the circumstances, however, I thought it wisest to accept his gift in your name and hope that you could find an amicable solution to our dilemma at a later date."

"I suppose you're...Hey! Wait a minute. We already have Massha and Tananda in residence. Won't they do?"

Guido gave his sigh again. "This possibility did indeed occur to me as well. Then I said to myself: 'Guido, do you really want to be the one to hang the label of moll on either Massha or Tananda, knowing those ladies as you do? Even if it will only be bantered around the Mob?' Viewed in that light, it was my decision to go along with Don Bruce's proposal and leave it to you to make the final decision...*Boss*."

I shot a sharp glance at him for that last touch of sarcasm. Despite his affected speech patterns and pseudo-pompous explanations, I occasionally had the

28

impression that Guido was far more intelligent than he let on. At the moment, however, his face was a study in innocence, so I let it ride.

"I see what you mean, Guido. If either Massha or Tananda are going to be known as 'molls,' I'd rather it was their choice, not mine. Until then, I guess we're stuck with...what's her name? Bunny? Does she wiggle her nose or something?"

Guido glanced across the room at the other two, then lowered his voice conspiratorily. "Just between you and me, Boss, I think you would be well advised to accept this particular moll that Don Bruce has personally selected to send. Know what I mean?"

"No, I don't." I grimaced. "Excuse me, Guido, but the mind's working a little slow just now. If you're trying to tell me something, you're going to have to spell it out."

"Well, I did a little checkin' around, and it seems that Bunny here is Don Bruce's niece, and..."

"HIS N..."

"Ssshh. Keep it down, Boss. I don't think we're supposed to know that."

With a supreme effort, I suppressed my hysteria and lowered my voice again. "What are you trying to do to me? I'm trying to keep this operation under wraps and you bring me Don Bruce's niece?"

"Don't worry..."

"DON'T..."

"Sshh! Like I said, I've been checking around. It seems the two of them don't get along at all. Wouldn't give each other the time of day. The way I hear it, he doesn't want her to be a moll, and she won't go along with any other kind of work. They fight over it like cats and dogs. Anyway, if you can trust any moll to not feed Don Bruce the straight scoop, it's her. That's why I was sayin' that you should keep this one."

My headache had now spread to my stomach.

"Swell. Just swell. Well, at least . . ."

"The one thing I couldn't find out, though," Guido continued with a frown, "is why he wants her with you. I figure that it's either that he thinks that you'll treat her right, or that he expects you to scare her out of bein' a moll. I'm just not sure which way you should play it."

This was not turning out to be a good night for me. In fact, it had gone steadily downhill since I won that last hand of dragon poker.

"Guido," I said. "Please don't say anything more. Okay? Please? Every time I think that things might not be so bad, you drag out something else that makes them worse."

"Just tryin' to do my job," he shrugged, obviously hurt, "but if that's what you want . . . well, you're the Boss."

"And if you say that one more time, I'm liable to forget you're bigger than me and pop you one in the nose. Understand? Being the 'Boss' implies a certain degree of control, and if there's one thing I don't have right now, it's control."

"Right, B . . . Skeeve," my bodyguard grinned. "You know, for a minute there you sounded just like my old B . . . employer. He used to beat up on Nunzio and me when he got mad. Of course, we had to stand there and take it . . . ."

"Don't give me any ideas," I snarled. "For now, let's just concentrate on Bunny."

I turned my attention once more to the problem at hand, which was to say Bunny. She was still staring vacantly around the room, jaws working methodically on whatever it was she was chewing, and apparently oblivious to whatever it was Nunzio was trying to tell her.

"Well, uh . . . Bunny," I said, "it looks like you're going to be staying with us for a while."

She reacted to my words as if I had hit her "on" switch.

"Eeoooh!" she squealed, as if I had just told her that she had won a beauty pageant. "Oh, I know I'm just goin' to *love* workin' under you, Skeevie."

My stomach did a slow roll to the left.

"Shall I get her things, Boss?" Nunzio said. "She's got about a mountain and a half of luggage outside."

"Oh, you can leave all that," Bunny cooed. "I just know my Skeevie is going to want to buy me a whole new wardrobe."

"Hold it! Time out!" I ordered. "House rules time. Bunny, some things are going to disappear from your vocabulary *right now*. First, forget 'Skeevie.' It's Skeeve...just Skeeve, or if you must, the Great Skeeve in front of company. Not Skeevie."

"Gotcha," she winked.

"Next, you do not work *under* me. You're...you're my personal secretary. Got it?"

"Why sure, sugar. That's what I'm always called."

Again with the wink.

"Now then, Nunzio. I want you to get her luggage and move it into...I don't know, the pink bedroom."

"You want I should give him a hand, Boss?" Guido asked.

"*You* stay put." I smiled, baring all my teeth. "I've got a special job for you."

"Now just a darn minute!" Bunny interrupted, her cutie-pie accent noticeably lacking. "What's this with the 'pink bedroom'? Somehow you don't strike me as the kind that sleeps in a pink bedroom. Aren't I moving into your bedroom?"

"*I'm* sleeping in my bedroom," I said. "Now isn't it easier for you to move into one of our spares than for me to relocate just so you can move into mine?"

As I said, it had been a long night, and I was more than a little slow. Lucky for me, Bunny was fast enough for both of us.

"I thought we was goin' to be sharin' a room, Mr.

Skeeve. That's the whole idea of my bein' here, ya know? What's wrong? Ya think I got bad breath or sumpin'?"

"Aahh...ummm..." I said intelligently.

"Hi, Guido...Nunzio. Who's...oh wow!"

That last witty line didn't come from me. Massha had just entered the room with Markie in tow and lurched to a halt at the sight of Bunny.

"Hey, Boss! What's with the kid?"

"Guido, Nunzio, this is Markie...our *other* house guest. Massha, Markie, this is Bunny. She's going to be staying with us for a while...in the *pink* bedroom."

"Now I get it!" Bunny exclaimed. "You want we should play it cool because of the kid! Well, you can count on me. Discretion is Bunny's middle name. The pink bedroom it is!"

I could cheerfully have throttled her. If her meaning was lost on Markie, it certainly hadn't gotten past Massha, who was staring out at me from under raised eyebrows.

"Whatever!" I said rather than take more drastic action. "Now, Nunzio, you get Bunny set up in the pink bedroom. Massha, I want you to get Markie settled in the blue bedroom next to mine...and knock it off with the eyebrows. I'll explain everything in the morning."

"*That* I want to hear," she snorted. "C'mon, kid."

"I'm not tired!" Markie protested.

"Tough!" I countered. "I am."

"Oh," she said meekly and followed Massha.

Whatever kind of a crumb her father might be, somewhere along the line she had learned when adults could be argued with and when it was best to go with the flow.

"What do you want me to do, Boss?" Guido asked eagerly.

I favored him with my evilest grin.

"Remember that special assignment I said I had for you?"

"Yea, Boss?"

"I'll warn you, it's dangerous."

That appealed to his professional pride, and he puffed out his chest. "The tougher the better. You know me!"

"Fine," I said. "All you have to do is go upstairs and explain Bunny to Aahz. It seems my partner isn't talking to me just now."

Chapter V

"Such stuff dreams are made of."
S. Beauty

L<small>UANNA</small> WAS with me. I couldn't remember
when she arrived or how long she had been here, but I
didn't care. I hadn't seen her since we got back from the
jailbreak on Limbo, and I had missed her terribly. She
had left me to stay with her partner, Matt, and a little
piece of me went with her. I won't be so cornball as to say
it was my heart, but it was in that general vicinity.

There was so much I wanted to tell her...wanted
to ask her, but it didn't really seem necessary. We just
lay side by side on a grassy hill watching the clouds,
enjoying each other's company in silence. I could have
stayed like that forever, but she raised herself on one
elbow and spoke softly to me.

"If you'll just skootch over a little, Skeevie, we can
both get comfy."

34

This was somehow jarring to my serenity. She didn't sound like Luanna at all. Luanna's voice was musical and exciting. She sounded like...

"BUNNY!"

I was suddenly sitting bolt upright, not on a grassy knoll, but in my own bed.

"Ssshh! You'll wake up the kid!"

She was perched on the edge of my bed wearing something filmy that was even more revealing than the skin-tight outfit she had had on last night.

"What are you doing in my room!?"

I had distinct memories of stacking several pieces of furniture in front of the door before I retired, and a quick glance confirmed that they were still in place.

"Through the secret passageway," she said with one of her winks. "Nunzio showed it to me last night."

"Oh, he did, did he?" I snarled. "Remind me to express my thanks to him for that little service."

"Save your thanks, sugar. You're goin' to need them when I get done with you."

With that she raised the covers and slid in next to me. I slid out the other side of the bed as if a spider had just joined me. Not that I'm afraid of spiders, mind you, but Bunny scares me stiff.

"Now what's wrong?" she whined.

"Um...ah...look, Bunny. Can we talk for a minute?"

"Sure," she said, sitting up in bed and bending forward to rest her elbows on her knees. "Anything you say."

Unfortunately, her current position also gave me an unrestricted view of her cleavage. I promptly forgot what I was going to say.

"Aaah...I...um..."

There was a knock at the door.

"Come in!" I said, grateful for the interruption.

That is beyond a doubt the dumbest thing I have

ever said.

The door opened, sweeping the stacked furniture back with amazing ease, and Chumley walked in.

"I say, Skeeve, Aahz has just been telling me the most remarkable...Hal-lo?"

I mentioned before that Chumley is a troll. What I didn't say was that he could blush...probably because I didn't know it myself until just now. Of all the sights I've seen in several dimensions, a blushing troll is in a category all its own.

"You must be Chumley!" Bunny chirped. "The boys told me about you."

"Umm...quite right. Pleased to make your acquaintance and all that," the troll said, trying to avert his eyes while still making polite conversation.

"Yeah. Sure, Chum. Don't you have somethin' else to do...like leavin'?"

I clutched at his arm in desperation.

"No! I mean...Chumley always comes by first thing in the morning."

"Ahh...Yes. Just wanted to see if Skeeve was ready for a spot of breakfast."

"Well, I got here first," Bunny bristled. "If Skeevie wants something to nibble on, he can..."

"Good morning, Daddy!"

Markie came bounding into the room and gave me a hug before any of us knew she was around.

"Well, well. You must be Skeeve's new ward, Markie," the troll beamed, obviously thankful to have something to focus on other than Bunny.

"And you're Chumley. Hi, Bunny!"

"Hiya, kid," Bunny responded with a noticeable lack of enthusiasm as she pulled the covers up around her neck.

"Are you up, Skeeve?"

The voice wafting in from the corridor was immediately identifiable as Tananda.

Chumley and I had rarely worked together as a team, but this time no planning or coordination was necessary. I scooped Markie up and carried her into the hall while Chumley followed, slamming the door behind him with enough force to crack the wood.

"Pip pip, little sister. Fine day, isn't it?"

"Hi, Tananda! What's new?"

Our cordial greetings, intended to disarm the situation, succeeded only in stopping our colleague in her tracks.

Tananda is quite attractive—if curvaceous, olive-skinned, green-haired women are your type. Of course, she looks a lot better when she isn't pursing her lips and narrowing her eyes suspiciously.

"Well, for openers, I'd say the little girl under your arm is new," she said firmly. "I may not be the most observant person, but I'm sure I would have noticed her if she had been around before."

"Oh. Well, there are a few things I've got to debrief you on," I smiled weakly. "This is one of them. Her name is Markie, and..."

"Later, Skeeve. Right now I'm more curious about what my big brother's up to. How 'bout it, Chumley? I've seen you slam doors on the way *into* bedrooms before, but never on the way out."

"Ummm...that is..." the troll mumbled awkwardly.

"Actually," I assisted, "it's more like...you see..."

"Exactly what I had in mind," Tananda declared, slipping past us and flinging the bedroom door open.

My room was mercifully empty of occupants. Apparently Bunny had retreated through whatever secret panel she had emerged from. Chumley and I exchanged unnoted glances of relief.

"I don't get it," Tananda frowned. "You two acted like you were trying to hide a body. There's nothing here to be so secretive about."

"I think they didn't want you to see the girl in my daddy's bed," Markie supplied brightly.

I wanted to express my thanks to Markie but decided that I had enough problems without adding murder to the list.

"Well, Skeeve?" Tananda said, her eyebrows almost reaching her hairline.

"Ummm...actually, I'm not really her daddy. That's one of the things I wanted to debrief you about."

"I meant about the girl in your room!"

"That's the other thing I wanted to..."

"Cut him some slack! Huh, Tananda? It's uncivilized to beat up on someone before breakfast."

That was Aahz, who for once had approached our gathering without being seen...or heard. He's usually not big on quiet entrances.

For that matter, I had never known him to be at all reluctant about beating up on someone—say, for example, me—before breakfast. Still, I was grateful for his intervention.

"Hi, Aahz. We were just..."

"Do you know what your partner is doing!?" Tananda said in a voice that could freeze wine. "He *seems* to be turning our home into a combination day-care center and..."

"I know all about it," Aahz interrupted, "and so will you if you'll just cool down. We'll explain everything over breakfast."

"Well..."

"Besides," Markie piped up, "it's not *your* home. It's my daddy's. He just lets you live here. He can do anything he wants in *his* house!"

I released my hold on her, hoping to dump her on her head. Instead, she twisted in midair and landed on her feet like a cat, all the while sneering smugly.

Tananda had stiffened as if someone had jabbed her with a pin.

"I suppose you're right, Markie," she said through tight lips. "If the 'Great Skeeve' wants to romp with some bit of fluff, it's none of my business. And if I don't like it, I should just go elsewhere."

She spun on her heel and started off down the hall.

"What about breakfast?" Aahz called after her.

"I'll be eating out...permanently!"

We watched her departure in helpless silence.

"I'd better go after her," Chumley said at last. "In the mood she's in, she might hurt someone."

"Could you take Markie with you?" Aahz requested, still staring after Tananda.

"Are you kidding?" the troll gaped.

"Well, at least drop her off in the kitchen. I've got to have a few words with Skeeve in private."

"I want to stay here!" Markie protested.

"Go," I said quietly.

There must have been something in my voice, because both Markie and Chumley headed off without further argument.

"Partner, you've got a problem."

"Don't I know it. If there was any way I could ship her back to Don Bruce, I'd do it in a minute, but..."

"I'm not talking about Bunny!"

That stopped me.

"You aren't?"

"No. Markie's the problem, not Bunny."

"Markie? But she's just a little girl."

Aahz heaved a small sigh and put one hand on my shoulder...gently, for a change.

"Skeeve, I've given you a lot of advice in the past, some of it better than others. For the most part, you've done pretty well at winging it in unfamiliar situations, but this time you're in over your head. Believe me, you don't have the vaguest idea of the kind of havoc a kid can cause in your life...especially a little girl."

I didn't know what to say. My partner was obviously

sincere in his concern, and for a change was expressing it in a very calm, low-key manner. Still, I couldn't go along with what he was saying.

"C'mon, Aahz. How much trouble can she be? This thing with Tananda happened because of Bunny..."

"...after Markie started mouthing off at the wrong time. I already had Tananda cooling off when Markie put her two cents in."

It also occurred to me that Markie was the one who had spilled the beans to Tananda in the first place. I shoved that thought to the back of my mind.

"So she doesn't have enough sense to keep her mouth shut. She's just a kid. We can't expect her to..."

"That's my point. Think about our operation for a minute, partner. How many times in one day can things go sour if someone says the wrong thing at the right moment? It's taken us a year to get Guido and Nunzio on board...and they're adults. Bringing a kid into the place is like waving a torch around a fireworks factory."

As much as I appreciated his efforts to explain a problem to me, I was starting to weary a bit of Aahz's single-minded pursuit of his point.

"Okay. So I haven't had much experience around kids. I may be underestimating the situation, but aren't you being a bit of an alarmist? What experience are you basing *your* worries on?"

"Are you kidding?" my partner said, laughing for the first time in our conversation. "Anyone who's been around as many centuries as I have has had more than their share of experience with kids. You met my nephew Rupert? You think he was born an adult? And he's only one of more nieces, nephews, and grandchildren than I can count without being reduced to a nervous wreck by the memories."

And I thought I couldn't be surprised by Aahz any more.

"Really? Grandchildren? I never even knew you

had kids."

"I don't like to talk about it. That in itself should be a clue. When someone who likes to talk as much as I do totally avoids a subject, the memories have got to be less than pleasant!"

I was starting to get a bit worried. Realizing that Aahz usually tends to minimize danger, his warnings were starting to set my overactive imagination in gear.

"I hear what you're saying, Aahz. But we're only talking about one kid here. How much trouble can one little girl be?"

My partner's face suddenly split into one of his infamous evil grins. "Remember that quote," he said. "I'm going to be tossing it back at you from time to time."

"But..."

"Hey, Boss! There's someone here to see you!"

Just what I needed! I had already pretty much resolved not to take on any more clients until after Markie's father had reclaimed her. Of course, I didn't want to say that in front of Aahz, especially considering our current conversation.

"I'm in the middle of a conference, Guido!" I called. "Tell them to come back later."

"Suit yourself, Boss!" came the reply. "I just thought you'd want to know, seein' as how it's Luanna...."

I was off like a shot, not even bothering to excuse myself. Aahz would understand. He knew I'd had a thing for Luanna since our expedition into Limbo.

On my way to the waiting room, I had time to speculate as to whether or not this was one of my bodyguard's little pranks. I decided that if it was, I would study hard until I knew enough magic to turn him into a toad.

My suspicions were groundless. She was there. My beautiful blond goddess. What really made my heart leap, though, was that she had her luggage with her.

"Hi, Luanna. What are you doing here? Where's Matt? How have things been? Would you like something to drink? Could I..."

I suddenly realized that I was babbling and forced myself to pause.

"Aahh...what I'm trying to say is that it's good to see you."

That got me the slow smile that had haunted my dreams. "I'm glad, Skeeve. I was afraid you'd forgotten about me."

"Not a chance," I said, then realized I was leering. "That is, no, I haven't forgotten a thing about you."

Her deep blue eyes locked with mine, and I felt myself sinking helplessly into their depths.

"That's good," she said in that musical voice of hers. "I was worried about taking you up on your offer after all this time."

That got through the fog that was threatening to envelop my mind. "Offer? What offer?"

"Oh, you don't remember! I thought...oh, this is embarrassing."

"Wait a minute!" I cried. "I haven't forgotten! It's just that...let me think...it's just..."

Like a beam of sunlight in a swamp the memory came to me. "You mean when I said that you could come to work for Aahz and me? That's it? Right?"

"That's what I was talking about!" The sun came from behind the clouds as she smiled again. "You see, Matt and I have split, and I thought..."

"Do you want any breakfast, Daddy? You said... oh! Hello."

"DADDY!!??"

Markie and Luanna stared at each other.

I revised my plans rapidly. I would study hard and turn *myself* into a toad.

"I can explain, Luanna..." I began.

"I think you should keep this one, Daddy," Markie said, never taking her eyes off Luanna. "She's a lot prettier than the other one."

"THE OTHER...Oh! You mean Tananda."

"No, I mean..."

"MARKIE!" I interrupted desperately. "Why don't you wait for me in the kitchen. I'll be along in a minute after I finish talking to..."

"Skeevie, are we going to go shopping?" Bunny slithered into the room. "I need...who's that!?"

"Me? I'm nobody." Luanna responded grimly. "I never realized until just now how much of a nobody I am!"

"Well, the job's already taken, if that's what you're here for," Bunny smirked.

"Wait a minute! It's a different job! Really! Luanna, I can...Luanna??"

Sometime during my hysteria, the love of my life had gathered up her bags and left. I was talking to empty air.

"Gee, Skeevie. What're you talkin' to her for when you got me? Aren't I..."

"Daddy. Can I..."

"SHUT UP! BOTH OF YOU! Let me think!"

Try as I might, the only thought that kept coming to me was that maybe Aahz was right. Maybe kids were more trouble than I thought.

Chapter VI

*"Bring the whole family . . . but
leave the kids at home!"*
R. McDonald

REALLY, Hot Stuff. Do you think this is such a
great idea?"

"Massha, please! I'm trying to think things out.
I couldn't get my thoughts together back at
Chaos Central with Aahz nattering at me, and I won't be
able to do it now if you start up. Now, are you going to
help or not?"

My apprentice shrugged her massive shoulders.
"Okay. What do you want me to do?"

"Just keep an eye on those two and see that they
don't get into any trouble while I think."

"Keep them out of trouble? At the Bazaar at Deva?
Aren't Guido and Nunzio supposed to . . ."

"Massha!"

"All right. All right. I want it noted, though, that I'm taking this assignment under protest."

I'm *sure* I didn't give Aahz this much back talk when I was apprenticed to him. Every time I say that out loud, however, my partner bursts into such gales of laughter that now I tend to keep the thought to myself, even when he isn't around.

After some resistance, I had agreed to take Bunny and Markie on a stroll through the Bazaar. As I said to Massha, this was more to get a bit of time away from Aahz than it was giving in to Bunny's whining, though that voice was not easy to ignore.

In acknowledgment of Aahz's repeated warnings of trouble, I had recruited my apprentice to accompany us so I'd have a backup if things went awry. Guido and Nunzio were along, of course, but they were more concerned with things coming at me than with anything anyone in our party might do to the immediate environment.

All in all, we made quite a procession. Two Mob bodyguards, a woman-mountain disguised as a jewelry display, a moll, a kid, and me! For a change, I wasn't the "kid" of the party. There was something to be said for having an honest-to-goodness child traveling with you. It automatically made one look older and somehow more responsible.

We had been in residence at the Bazaar for some time now, and the neighborhood merchants were pretty much used to us. That is, they knew that if I was interested, I'd come to them. If I wasn't, no amount of wheedling or cajoling would tempt me into buying. That might seem a little strange to you, after all my glowing accounts of the wonders for sale at the Bazaar, but I had fallen into the pattern quite naturally. You see, if you just visit the Bazaar once in a while, it's all quite impressive, and you feel compelled to buy just to keep from losing out on some really nifty bargains. If you live there, on the other hand, there's no real compulsion to buy anything right now. I mean, if I need a plant that grows ten feet in a minute, I'll buy it...when I need it. Until then, the plant can stay in its shop three doors from our tent, and my money can stay in my pocket.

That's how things were, normally. Of course, my situation today was anything but normal. I had known this all along, of course, but I hadn't really stopped to think through all the ramifications of my current state of affairs.

Okay. So I was dumb. Remember, I was taking this stroll to try to get a chance to think. Remember?

Maybe I hadn't zeroed in on what my party looked like, but the Deveels spotted the difference before we had gone half a block.

Suddenly, every Deveel who hadn't been able to foist off some trinket on me for the last two years was out to give it one more try.

"Love potions! Results guaranteed!"

"Snake necklaces! Poisonous and non!"

"Special discounts for the Great Skeeve!"

"Special discounts for any *friend* of the Great Skeeve!"

"Try our..."

"Buy my..."

"Taste these..."

Most of this was not aimed at me, but at Bunny and Markie. The Deveels swarmed around them like...well, like Deveels smelling an easy profit. This is not to say that Guido and Nunzio weren't doing their jobs. If they hadn't been clearing a path for us, we wouldn't have been able to move at all. As it was, our progress was simply slowed to a crawl.

"Still think this was a good idea, High Roller?"

"Massha! If you..."

"Just asking. If you can think in this racket, though, you've got better concentration than I do."

She was right, but I wasn't about to admit it. I just kept staring forward as we walked, tracking the activity around me out of the corners of my eyes without turning my head.

"Skeevie! Can I have..."

"No."

"Look at..."

"No."

"Couldn't we..."

"No!"

Bunny was getting to be a pain. She seemed to want everything in sight. Fortunately, I had developed the perfect defense. All I had to do was say "No!" to everything.

"Why did we go shopping if we aren't going to buy anything?"

"Well..."

So much for my perfect defense. Not to be stymied, I switched immediately to Plan B, which was simply to keep our purchases at a minimum. I didn't seem to be too successful at that, either, but I consoled myself by trying to imagine how much junk we would have gotten loaded down with if I hadn't been riding the brake.

Surprisingly enough, despite all of Aahz's dire predictions, Markie wasn't much trouble at all. I found her to be remarkably well mannered and obedient, and she never asked me to buy her anything. Instead, she contented herself with pointing out to Bunny the few booths that individual overlooked.

There weren't many.

My only salvation was that Bunny did not seem interested in the usual collection of whiz-bangs and wowers that most visitors to the Bazaar find irresistible. She was remarkably loyal to her prime passion— apparel. Hats, dresses, shoes, and accessories all had to pass her close scrutiny.

I'll admit that Bunny did not indulge in random

purchases. She had a shrewd eye for fabric and construction, and better color sense than anyone I have ever known. Aahz always said that Imps were flashy dressers, and I had secretly tried to pattern my own wardrobe after their example. However, one afternoon of shopping with Bunny was an education in itself. Imps have nothing on molls when it comes to clothes sense.

The more I watched Bunny peruse the fashions available at the Bazaar, the more self-conscious I became about my own appearance. Eventually, I found myself looking over a few items for myself, and from there it was a short step to buying.

In no time flat, we had a small mountain of packages to cart along with us. Bunny had stocked up on a couple of outfits that changed color with her mood, and was now wearing an intriguing blouse which had a transparent patch that migrated randomly around her torso. If the latter sounds distracting, it was. My own indulgences were few, but sufficient to add to the overall bulk of merchandise we had to transport.

Guido and Nunzio were exempt from package-carrying duties, and Massha flatly refused on the basis that being a large woman trying to maneuver through the Bazaar was difficult enough without trying to juggle packages at the same time. Realizing the "you break it, you bought it" policies of the Bazaar, I could scarcely argue with her cautious position.

The final resolution to our baggage problem was really quite simple. I flexed my magic powers a bit and levitated the whole kit and kaboodle. I don't normally like to flaunt my powers publicly, but I figured that this was a necessary exception to the rule. Of course, having our purchases floating along behind us was like having a lighthouse in tow; it drew the Deveels out of their stalls in droves.

To my surprise, I started to enjoy the situation. Humility and anonymity is well and good, but sometimes its nice to be made a fuss over. Bunny hung on my arm and shoulder like a boneless falcon, cooing little endearments of appreciation...though the fact that I was willing to finance her purchases seemed to be making as much as or more of an impression on her than my minor display of magic.

"Can't say I think much of her taste in clothes," Massha murmured to me as we paused once more while Bunny darted into a nearby booth.

To say the least, I was not eager to get drawn into a discussion comparing the respective tastes in clothes of Bunny and my apprentice.

"Different body types look better in different styles," I said, as tactfully as I could.

"Yeah? And what style looks best on *my* body type?"

"In all honesty, Massha, I can't picture you dressing any differently than you do."

"Really? Say, thanks, Skeeve. A girl always likes to hear a few appreciative noises about how she looks."

I had narrowly sidestepped that booby-trap and cast about frantically for a new subject before the other interpretation of my statement occurred to her.

"Umm...hasn't Markie been well-behaved?"

"I'll say. I'll admit I was a little worried when you first brought her in, but she's been an angel. I don't think I've ever known a kid this patient and obedient."

"Undemanding, too," I said. "I've been thinking of getting her something while we're out, but I'm having trouble coming up with anything appropriate. The Bazaar isn't big on toy shops."

"Are you kidding? It's one big toy shop!"

"Massha..."

"Okay, okay. So they're mostly toys for adults. Let me think. How old is she, anyway?"

"I'm not really sure. She said she was in the third grade at Elementary School...even though she calls it Elemental School...so that would make her..."

50

I realized that Massha was staring at me in wide-eyed horror.

"Elemental School!?"

"That's what she called it. Cute, huh? Why, what does..."

My apprentice interrupted me by grabbing my arm so hard that it hurt. "Skeeve. We've got to get her back home...QUICK!!"

"But I don't see..."

"I'll explain later! Just get her and go! I'll round up Bunny and get her back, but you've got to get moving!"

To say the least, I found her manner puzzling. I had never seen Massha so upset. This was obviously not the time for questions, though, so I looked around for Markie.

She was standing, fists clenched, glaring at a tent with a closed flap.

All of a sudden everyone was getting uptight. First Massha, and now Markie.

"What's with the kid?" I said, tapping Guido on the shoulder.

"Bunny's in trying on some peek-a-boo nighties, and the owner chased Markie out," my bodyguard explained. "She don't like it much, but she'll get over it. It's part of bein' a kid, I guess."

"I see. Well, I was just going to take her back home anyway. Could one of you stay with..."

"SKEEVE! STOP HER!!"

Massha was shouting at me. I was turning toward her to see what she was talking about when it happened, so I didn't see all the details.

There was a sudden WHOOSH followed by the sounds of ripping canvas, wood splintering, and assorted screams and curses.

I whipped my head back around, and my jaw dropped in astonishment.

The booth that Bunny was in was in tatters. The

entire stock of the place was sailing off over the Bazaar, as was what was left of the tent. Bunny was trying to cover herself with her hands and screaming her head off. The proprietor, a particularly greasy-looking Deveel, was also screaming his head off, but his emotions were being vented in our general direction instead of at the world in general.

I would say it was a major dilemma except for one thing. The displays on either side of Bunny's tent and for two rows behind it were in a similar state. *That* is a major dilemma, making the destruction of a single booth pale in comparison.

A voice sprang into my head, drowning out the clamor of the enraged merchants. "If you break it, you bought it!" the voice said, and it spoke with a Devan accent.

"What happened?" I gasped, though whether to myself or to the gods, I wasn't sure.

Massha answered.

"What happened was Markie!" she said grimly. "She blew her cork and summoned up an air elemental...you know, like you learn to do at *Elemental School?* It appears that when the kid throws a tantrum, she's going to do it with magic!"

My mind grasped the meaning of her words instantly, just as fast as it leaped on to the next plateau. Aahz! I wasn't sure which was going to be worse: breaking the news to Aahz, or telling him how much it had cost us to learn about it!

Chapter VII

*"There's a time to fight, and
a time to hide out!"*

B. Cassidy

I'VE HEARD that when some people get depressed, they retire to their neighborhood bar and tell their troubles to a sympathetic bartender. The problem with the Bazaar at Deva (a problem I had never noticed before) is that there are no sympathetic bartenders!

Consequently, I had to settle for the next best thing and holed up in the Yellow Crescent Inn.

Now, a fast-food joint may seem to you to be a poor substitute for a bar. It is. This particular fast-food joint, however, is owned and managed by my only friend at the Bazaar who isn't living with me. This last part was especially important at the moment, since I didn't think I was apt to get much sympathy in my own home.

Gus is a gargoyle, but despite his fierce appearance

he's one of the friendliest beings I've ever met. He's helped Aahz and me out on some of our more dubious assignments, so he's less inclined to ask "How did you get yourself into this?" than most. Usually, he's more interested in "How do you get out of it?".

"How did you get yourself into this one?" he said, shaking his head.

Well, nobody's perfect...especially friends.

"I *told* you, Gus. One lousy card game where I expected to lose. If I had known it was going to backfire like this, so help me I would have folded every hand!"

"You see, there's your problem," the gargoyle said, flashing a grin toothier than normal. "Instead of sitting in and losing, you'd be better off not sitting in at all!"

I rewarded his sound advice by rolling my eyes.

"It's all hypothetical anyway. What's done is done. The question is, 'What do I do now?'"

"Not so fast. Let's stick with the card game for a minute. Why did you sit in if you were expecting to lose?"

"Look. Can we drop the card game? I was wrong. Okay? Is that what you want to hear?"

"No-o-o," Gus said slowly. "I still want to hear why you went in the first place. Humor me."

I stared at him for a moment, but he seemed perfectly serious.

I shrugged. "The Geek sent me an invitation. Frankly, it was quite flattering to get one. I just thought it would be sociable to..."

"Stop!" the gargoyle interrupted, raising his hand. "There's your problem."

"What is?"

"Trying to be sociable. What's the matter? Aren't your current round of friends good enough for you?"

That made me a little bit nervous. I was having enough problems without having Gus get his nose out of joint.

"It isn't that, Gus. Really. The whole crew—yourself included—is closer to me than my family ever was. It's just...I don't know..."

"...you want to be liked. Right?"

"Yeah. I guess that's it."

"And that's your problem!"

That one threw me.

"I don't get it," I admitted.

The gargoyle sighed, then ducked behind the counter. "Have another milkshake," he said, shoving one toward me. "This might take a while, but I'll try to explain."

I like to think it's a sign of my growing savoir-faire that I now enjoy strawberry milkshakes. When I first visited the Bazaar, I rejected them out of hand because they looked like pink swamp muck. I was now moderately addicted to them, though I still wouldn't eat the food here. Then again, maybe it was a sign of something else completely if I thought a taste for strawberry milkshakes was a sign of savoir-faire!

"Look, Skeeve," Gus began, sipping at a milkshake of his own, "you're a nice guy...one of the nicest I've ever known. You go out of your way to 'do the right thing'...to be nice to people. The key phrase there is 'go out of your way.' You're in a 'trouble-heavy' profession anyway. Nobody hires a magician because things are going well. Then you add to that your chosen lifestyle. Because you want to be liked, you place yourself in situations you wouldn't go near if it was for your own personal satisfaction. Case in point: the card game. If you had been out for personal gain, i.e., wealth, you wouldn't have gone near it, since you don't know the game. But you wanted to be friendly, so you went expecting to lose. That's not normal, and it resulted in a not-normal outcome, to wit, Markie. That's why you get into trouble."

I chewed my lip slightly as I thought over what he

was saying.

"So if I want to stay out of trouble, I've got to stop being a nice guy? I'm not sure I can do that, Gus."

"Neither am I," the gargoyle agreed cheerfully. "What's more, if you could, I don't think I or any of your other friends would like you any more. I don't even think you'd like yourself."

"Then why are you recommending that I change?"

"I'm not! I'm just pointing out that it's the way you are, not any outside circumstances, that keeps getting you into trouble. In short, since you aren't going to change, get used to being in trouble. It's going to be your constant state for a long while."

I found myself massaging my forehead again.

"Thanks, Gus," I said. "I knew I could count on you to cheer me up."

"Don't knock it. Now you can focus on solving your current problem instead of wasting time wondering why it exists."

"Funny. I thought I was doing just that. Someone *else* wanted to talk about what was causing my problems."

My sarcasm didn't faze the gargoyle in the least.

"Right," he nodded. "That brings us to your current problem.'

"Now you're talking. What do you think I should do, Gus?"

"Beats me. I'd say you've got a real dilemma on your hands."

I closed my eyes as my headache hammered anew.

"I don't know what I'd do without you, Gus."

"Hey. Don't mention it. What are friends for? Whoops! Here comes Tananda!"

The other disadvantage to holing up at the Yellow Crescent Inn, besides the fact that it isn't a bar, is that it's located right across the street from my home. This is not good for someone who's trying to avoid his house-mates.

Fortunately, this was one situation I could handle with relative ease.

"Don't tell her I'm here, Gus," I instructed.

"But..."

Not waiting to hear the rest of his protest, I grabbed my milkshake, slipped into a chair at a nearby table, and set to work with a fast disguise spell. By the time Tananda hit the door, the only one she could see in the place besides Gus was a potbellied Deveel sipping on a strawberry milkshake.

"Hi, Gus!" she sang. "Have you seen Skeeve around?"

"He...aahh...was in earlier." The gargoyle carefully avoided the lie.

"Oh, well. I guess I'll just have to leave without saying goodbye to him, then. Too bad. We weren't on particularly good terms the last time I saw him."

"You're leaving?"

Gus said it before the words burst out of my own mouth, saving me from blowing my disguise.

"Yea. I figure it's about time I moved on."

"I...umm...have been hearing some strange things about my neighbors, but I've never been sure how much to believe," the gargoyle said thoughtfully. "This sudden departure wouldn't have anything to do with the new moll that's been foisted off on Skeeve, would it?"

"Bunny? Naw. I'll admit I was a bit out of sorts when I first heard about it, but Chumley explained the whole thing to me."

"Then what's the problem?"

Gus was doing a terrific job of beating me to my lines. As long as he kept it up, I'd be able to get all my questions answered without revealing myself.

It had occurred to me to confront Tananda directly as soon as I heard what she was up to, but then I realized that this was a rare chance to hear her thoughts when she didn't think I was around.

"Well, it's something Markie said...."

Markie again. I definitely owed Aahz an apology.

"...She made some crack about her daddy, that's Skeeve, letting me live there, and it got me to thinking. Things have been nice these last couple years...almost too nice. Since we haven't had to worry about overhead, Chumley and I haven't been working much. More important, we haven't been working at working. It's too easy to hang around the place and wait for something to come to us."

"Getting fat and lazy, huh?" Gus grinned.

"Something like that. Now, you know me, Gus. I've always been footloose and fancy free. Ready to follow a job or a whim at the drop of a hat. If anyone had suggested to me that I should settle down, I would have punched their lights out. Now all of a sudden, I've got a permanent address and family...family beyond Chumley, I mean. I hadn't realized how domestic I was getting until Skeeve showed up with Markie. A kid, even. When I first saw her, my first thought was that it would be nice to have a kid around the place! Now I ask you, Gus, does that sound like me?"

"No, it doesn't."

The gargoyle's voice was so quiet I scarcely recognized it as his.

"Right then I saw the handwriting on the wall. If I don't start moving again, I'm going to take root... permanently. You know, the worst thing is that I don't really want to go. That's the scariest part of all."

"I don't think Aahz or Skeeve want you to go either."

"Now don't you start on me, Gus. This is hard enough for me as it is. Like I said, they're family, but they're stifling me. I've got to get away, even if it's only for a little while, or I'm going to lose a part of me...forever."

60

"Well, if you've made up your mind...good luck."

"Thanks, Gus. I'll be in touch from time to time. Keep an eye on the boys in case they buy more trouble than they can sell."

"I don't think you have to worry about Chumley. He's pretty levelheaded."

"Chumley's not the one I'm worried about."

I thought that was going to be her parting shot, but she paused with one hand on the door.

"You know, it's probably just as well that I couldn't find Skeeve. I'm not sure I could have stuck to my guns in a face-to-face...but then again, maybe that's why I was looking for him."

I could feel Gus's eyes on me as she slipped out.

"I suppose it's pointless to ask why you didn't say something, *Mister* Skeeve."

Even though I had worried earlier about getting Gus angry with me, somehow it didn't matter anymore.

"At first it was curiosity," I said, letting my disguise slip away. "Then, I didn't want to embarrass her."

"And at the end there? When she flat-out said that you could talk her out of going? Why didn't you speak up then? Do you *want* her to disappear?"

I couldn't even manage a spark of anger. "You know better than that, Gus," I said quietly. "You're hurting and lashing out at whoever's handy, which happens to be me. I didn't try to get her to stay for the same reason you didn't try harder. She feels we're stifling her, and if she wants out, it'd be pretty small of us to try to keep her for our own sakes, wouldn't it?"

There was prolonged silence, which was fine by me. I didn't feel much like talking anymore.

Rising, I started for the door.

"You were looking the other way when she left," the gargoyle said. "You might like to know there were tears in her eyes."

"Mine too," I replied without turning. "That's why I was looking the other way."

Chapter VIII

"What did I do wrong?"
Lear, Rex

WITH A HEAVY heart, I headed back home. I was no longer worried about Aahz yelling at me. If anything, I was rather hoping he would. If he did, I decided that for a change I wouldn't even argue back. In short, I felt terrible and was in the mood to do a little penance.

Sliding through the tent flap, I cocked an ear and listened for Aahz. Actually, I was a little surprised that I couldn't hear him from the street, but I was sure I would be able to locate his position in the house with no difficulty. As I've said before, my partner has no problem expressing his moods, particularly anger.

The house was silent.

From the lack of reverberations and/or falling plaster, I assumed that Aahz was out . . . probably looking for me with blood in his eye. I debated going out to look

63

for him, but decided that it would be better to wait right here. He'd be back eventually, so I headed for the garden to make myself comfortable until he showed up.

What I call the garden is actually our courtyard. It has a fountain and an abundance of plants, so I tend to think of it as a piece of the outdoors rather than as an enclosed area. I had been spending more and more time there lately, especially when I wanted time to think. It reminded me of some of the quieter spots I would find from time to time back when I was living on my own in the woods...back before I met Garkin, and, through him, Aahz.

That memory led me to ponder a curious point: Were there other successful beings, like myself, who used their new prosperity to recreate the setting or atmosphere of their pre-success days? If so, it made for a curious cycle.

I was so preoccupied with this thought as I entered the garden that I almost missed the fact that I wasn't alone. Someone else was using my retreat...specifically, Aahz.

He was sitting on one of the stone benches, chin in his hands and elbows on his knees, staring blankly into the water as it flowed through the fountain.

To say the least, I was surprised. Aahz has never been the meditative type, particularly in times of crisis. He's more the "beat on someone or something until the problem goes away" type. Still, here he was, not agitated, not pacing, just sitting and staring. It was enough out of character for him to unnerve me completely.

"Umm...Hi, Aahz," I said hesitantly.

"Hello, Skeeve," he replied without looking around.

I waited for a few moments for him to say something else. He didn't. Finally I sat down on the bench next to him and stared at the water myself a bit.

We sat that way for a while, neither of us saying anything. The trickling water began to have a tranquil-

izing, hypnotic effect on me, and I found my mind starting to relax and drift.

"It's been quite a day, hasn't it, partner?"

My mind reflexively recoiled into a full defensive posture before it dawned on me that Aahz was still speaking quietly.

"Y...Yes."

I waited, but he seemed off in his own thoughts again. My nerves shot, I decided to take the initiative.

"Look, Aahz. About Markie..."

"Yes?"

"I knew about the Elemental School thing. She told me on the way back from the Geek's. I just didn't know enough to realize it was important."

"I know," Aahz sighed, not looking at me. "I hadn't bothered to teach you about elemental magic...just like I hadn't taught you about dragon poker."

No explosion! I was starting to get a little worried about my partner.

"Aren't you upset?"

"Of course I'm upset," he said, favoring me with a fleeting glimpse of bared teeth, a barely recognizable smile. "Do you think I'm always this jovial?"

"I mean, aren't you mad?"

"Oh, I'm past 'mad.' I'm all the way to 'thoughtful.'"

I arrived at the startling conclusion that I liked it better when Aahz was shouting and unreasonable. *That* I knew how to deal with. This latest mood of his was a total unknown.

"What are you thinking about?"

"Parenthood."

"Parenthood?"

"Yeah. You know, that state of total responsibility for another being? Well, at least, that's the theory."

I wasn't sure I was following this at all.

"Aahz? Are you trying to say you feel responsible for what happened with Markie because you hadn't taught me more about magic and poker?"

"Yes. No. I don't know."

"But that's silly!"

"I know," he replied, with his first honest grin since I had entered the garden. "That's what got me thinking about parenthood."

I abandoned any hope of following his logic.

"You'll have to explain it to me, Aahz. I'm a little slow today."

He straightened up a bit, draping one arm around my shoulders.

"I'll try, but it isn't easy," he said in a tone that was almost conversational. "You see, regardless of what I said when I was ranting at you about how much of a problem Markie was going to be, it's been a long time since I was a parent. I've been sitting here, trying to remember what it was like. What's so surprising to me is the realization that I've never really stopped. Nobody does."

I started to shift uncomfortably.

"Hear me out. For once I'm trying to share some of my hard-won lessons with you without shouting. Forget the theories of parenthood! What it's really all about is taking pride in things you can never be sure you had a hand in, and accepting the responsibility and guilt for things you either didn't know or had no control over. Actually, it's a lot more complicated than that, but that's the bare bones of the matter."

"You don't make it sound particularly attractive," I observed.

"In a lot of ways, it isn't. Your kid expects you to know everything...to be able to answer any question he asks and, more important, to provide a logical explanation of what is essentially an illogical world. Society, on the other hand, expects you to train your kid in everything necessary for them to become a successful, responsible member of the community...even if you aren't yourself. The problem is that you aren't the only source of input for the kid. Friends, schools, and other adults are all supplying other opinions, many of which you don't agree with. That means that if your kid succeeds, you don't really know if it was because of or in spite of your influence. On the other hand, if the kid goes bad, you always wonder if there was something else you could have said or done or done differently that could have salvaged things before they hit the wall."

His hand tightened slightly on my shoulder, but I don't think he did it consciously.

"Now, I wasn't a particularly good parent...which I like to think places me in the majority. I didn't interact much with my kids. Business was always a good excuse, but the truth was that I was glad to let someone else handle their upbringing as much as possible. I can see now that it was because I was afraid that if I tried to do it myself, that in my ignorance and uncertainty I would make some terrible mistake. The end result was that some of the kids turned out okay, some of them...let's say less than okay. What I was left with was a nagging feeling that I could have done better. That I could have—should have—made more of a difference."

He released his hold on my shoulders and stood up.

"Which brings us to you."

I wasn't sure if I should feel uncomfortable because he was focusing on me, or glad because he was pacing again.

"I've never consciously thought of you as a son, but in hindsight I realize that a lot of how I've treated you has been driven by my lingering guilt from parenthood. In you, I had another chance to mold someone...to give all the advice I felt I should have given my own kids. If at times I've seemed to overreact when things didn't go well, it's because deep inside I saw it as a personal failure. I mean, this was my second chance. A time to show how much I had learned from my earlier perceived failures, and you know what? Now I'm giving it my full attention and my best shot, and things are *still* going wrong!"

This was doing nothing to brighten my mood. On top of everything else, now I had the distinct feeling I had somehow let Aahz down.

"I don't think you can say it's your fault, Aahz. I mean, you've tried hard and been more patient with me than anyone I've ever known. Nobody can teach someone else everything, even if they could remember what should be taught. I've got a certain saturation point. After that, I'm not going to learn anything new until I've digested what I've got. Even then, I've got to be honest and say there are some things I don't believe no matter how often you tell me. I've just got to find out for myself. A craftsman can't blame his skill if he has defective material."

"That's just what I've been thinking," Aahz nodded. "I can't keep blaming myself for everything. It's very astute of you to have figured this out at your age... without going through what I have."

"It's no big thing to figure out that I'm a dummy," I said bitterly. "I've known it all along."

Suddenly, I felt myself being lifted into the air. I looked past Aahz's hand, which was gripping my shirt by the collar, down the length of his arm, and into his yellow eyes.

"Wrong lesson!" he snarled, sounding much like his old self. "What you're supposed to be learning isn't that you're dumb. You're not, and if you were listening, I just complimented you on that fact."

"Then what..." I managed, with what little air I had left.

"The point is that what's happened in the past isn't *my* fault, just like what's happening now isn't *your* fault!"

"Aaggh...urk..." was my swift rebuttal.

"Oh! Sorry."

My feet hit the floor and air flooded back into my lungs.

"All a parent, *any* parent, can do is give it their best shot, right or wrong." Aahz continued as if there had been no interruption. "The actual outcome rests on so many variables, no single person can assume responsibility, blame, or praise for whatever happens. That's important for me to remember in my dealings with you...and for you to remember in your dealings with Markie. It's not your fault!"

"It isn't?"

"That's right. We both have strong paternal streaks in us, though I don't know where you got yours from, but all we can do is our best. We'v got to remember not to try to shoulder the blame for what other people do...like Tananda."

That sobered me up again. "You know about that, huh?"

"Yeah. She told me to tell you goodbye if she didn't see you, but I guess you already know."

I simply nodded, unable to speak.

"I was already worried about how you were going to react to the problems with Markie, and when Tananda left I knew you were going to take it hard. I've been trying to find a way to show you that you aren't alone. Right or wrong, what you're feeling has been around for a long time."

"Thanks, Aahz."

"Has it helped at all?"

I thought for a moment.

"A bit."

My partner heaved another sigh.

"Well," he said, "I tried. That's what's important...
I think."

"Cheerio, chaps. How's every little thing?"

I glanced up to find Chumley striding toward us,

70

beaming merrily. "Oh. Hi, Chumley."

"I thought you'd like to know," the troll announced, "I think I've figured out a way to charge the damage Markie caused this afternoon back to the Mob as a business expense!"

"That's swell, Chumley," Aahz said dully.

"Yeah. Terrific."

"'Allo, 'allo?" he said, cocking his head at us. "Any time the two biggest hustlers at the Bazaar fail to get excited over money, there's got to be something wrong. Out with it now. What's troubling you?"

"Do you want to tell him, Aahz?"

"Well..."

"I say, this wouldn't be about little sister leaving the nest, would it? Oh, there's a giggle."

"You know?" I blinked.

"I can see you're all broken up over it," Aahz said in a dangerous tone.

"Tish tosh!" the troll exclaimed. "I don't see where it's anything to get upset about. Tananda's just settling things in her mind, is all. She's found that she likes something that goes against her self-image. It might take a few days, but eventually she'll figure out that it's not the end of the world. Everybody goes through it. It's called 'growing up.' If anything, I think it's bloody marvelous that she's finally having to learn that things don't stay the same forever."

"You do?" I was suddenly starting to feel better.

"Certainly. Why, in just the time we've been chumming around together, Aahz has changed, you've changed, so have I, though I don't tend to show it as dramatically as you two or little sister. You blokes have just got a bad case of the guilts. Poppycock! You can't take the blame for everything, you know."

"That's good advice," I said, standing up and stretching. "Why can't you ever give me good advice like that, partner?"

"Cause any fool can see it without being told," Aahz snarled, but there was a twinkle in his eye. "The problem is that Pervects aren't just any fool."

"Quite right," Chumley grinned. "Now how about joining me in a little Happy Hour spot of wine while I tell you how clever I am at saving you money."

"I'd rather you impressed us with a solution to our baby-sitting problems," my partner said grimly, heading for the lounge.

I followed in their wake, strangely happy. Things were back to normal...or as normal as they ever get around here. Between us, I was sure we could find a positive course of action. I mean, after all, how much trouble could one little girl...

That thought crumbled in front of an image of elemental-blown tents.

I resolved to do more listening than talking in the upcoming war council.

Chapter IX

"They never let you live it down.
One little mistake!"

Nero

Relaxing over drinks with Aahz and Chumley, I felt the tensions and depressions of the day slipping away. It was nice to know that when things really got tough, I had friends to help me solve my problems, however complex or apparently hopeless.

"Well, guys," I said, pouring another round of wine for everyone. "Any ideas as to what we should do?"

"Beats me," Chumley said, toying with his goblet.

"I still think it's *your* problem," Aahz announced, leaning back in his chair and grinning evilly. "I mean, after all, you got into it without our help."

Like I said, it's great to have friends.

"I can't say I go along with that, Aahz old boy," the troll said with a wave. "Although I'll admit it's tempting.

The unfortunate reality is that as long as we're living and working as closely as we are, his problems are our problems, don't you know?"

As much as I appreciated the fact that Chumley's logic was moving them closer to lending me assistance, I felt the need to defend myself a little.

"I'd like to think it's a two-way street, Aahz. I've gotten dragged into a few of *your* problems as well."

He started to snap back, then pursed his lips and returned his attention to his wine. "I'll avoid comparing lists of how often which of us has gotten us in how much trouble and simply concede the point. I guess that's part of what a partnership is all about. Sorry if I seem a little snorky from time to time, but I've never had a partner before. It takes getting used to."

"I say! Well said, Aahz!" Chumley applauded. "You know, you're getting more civilized every day."

"Let's not get too carried away just yet. How about you, Chumley? You and your sister have helped us out often enough, but I don't recall either of *you* bringing your problems home with you. Isn't that a little lopsided?"

"I've always figured it's our way of kicking in on the rent," the troll said casually. "If our problems ever start interfering with your work, then I'll figure we've overstayed our welcome."

This came as a total surprise to me. I realized with a start that I was usually so busy with my own life and problems that I never got around to asking much about the work Chumley and Tananda were doing.

"Whoa up a minute here," I said. "Are you two having problems I don't know about?"

"Well, it isn't all beer and skittles," the troll grimaced briefly. "The subject at hand, however, is *your* problems. There's nothing on my plate that has a higher priority just now, so let's get to work on the latest crisis, shall we? I suggest we all put on our thinking caps and

74

brainstorm a little. Let's just stare at the ceiling and each toss out ideas as they occur to us."

I made myself a little promise to return to the subject of Tananda and Chumley's problems at a later date, then joined the others in staring thoughtfully at the ceiling.

Time crawled along, and no one said anything.

"Well, so much for brainstorming," Aahz said, reaching for the wine again. "I'll admit I'm coming up blank."

"Perhaps it would help if we started by defining the problem," Chumley urged. "Now, as I see it, we have two problems: Markie and Bunny. We're going to have trouble figuring out what to do about Bunny until we find out what Don Bruce has up his sleeve, and we've got to come up with a way to keep Markie from totally disrupting our lives until her father comes to pick her up."

"*If* he picks her up," my partner corrected helpfully.

"I'll admit, I still don't know how you did so well in that game to end up with Markie in the first place," the troll said, cocking one outsized eye at me and ignoring Aahz.

"Dumb luck. . . with the emphasis on *dumb.*"

"That's not the way I heard it," Chumley smirked. "Whatever your method was, it was successful enough to make you the talk of the Bazaar."

"What!?" Aahz said, sitting up in his chair again.

"You would hear it yourself if you weren't spending all your time sulking in your room," the troll winked. "When I went out after little sister today, it seemed that all I was hearing about was the new dragon poker champion of Deva. Everybody's talking about the game, or what they've heard about the game. I suspect they're embellishing upon the facts, from some of the descriptions of the hands, but there are those who are taking it all as gospel."

I remembered then that when the game broke up,

the other players had been very enthusiastic about my playing. At the time, I had been worried about the secret of my night out reaching Aahz (which, you'll recall, it did before I got home). The troubles with Markie and Bunny had occupied my mind and time ever since, so I hadn't stopped to think of other potential repercussions of the game gossip. Now, however...

Aahz was out of his seat, pacing back and forth.

"Chumley, if what you're saying is true...are you following this, partner?"

"Too bloody well," I growled.

That got my partner to pause momentarily to roll his eyes.

"Watch yourself," he warned. "You're starting to talk like Chumley now."

"You want I should talk like Guido instead, know what I mean?"

"I don't understand," the troll interrupted. "Is something amiss?"

"We don't have two problems," Aahz announced. "We've got *three!* Markie, Bunny, *and* the rumor mill!"

"Gossip? How can that be a problem?"

"Think it through, Chumley," I said. "All I need right now is to have a bunch of hotshot dragon poker players hunting me up to see if I'm as good as everybody says."

"That's only part of it, partner," Aahz added. "This could hurt our business and public images as well."

I closed my eyes and sighed.

"Spell it out for me, Aahz. I'm still learning, remember?"

"Well, we already know your reputation at magic has been growing fast...almost too fast. The competition hates you because you're taking all the prime assignments. No big deal! Professional jealousy is the price of success in any field. There comes a time, however, when you can get too big too fast. Then it isn't just your rivals you worry about. Everybody wants you taken down a peg or two if for no other reason than to convince themselves that your success is abnormal... that they don't have to feel bad for not measuring up."

He paused to stare at me hard.

"I'm afraid this dragon poker thing just might push you into the second category. A lot of beings excel here at the Bazaar, but they're only noted in one field. The Geek, for example, is a recognized figure among the gamblers, but he doesn't have any reputation to speak of as a magician or merchant. People can accept that... work hard and you rise toward the top of your group. You, on the other hand, have just made a strong showing in a second profession. I'm afraid there's going to be some backlash."

"Backlash?" I echoed weakly.

"It's like I've been trying to tell you: people aren't going to want you to get too much above them. At the very least they might start boycotting our business. At most... well, there are ways of sabotaging other people's success."

"You mean they're going to..."

"That's enough!" Chumley declared, slapping his palm down on the table loudly.

It suddenly occurred to me that I had never seen Chumley mad. It also occurred to me that I was glad our furniture was strong enough to withstand even Aahz's tirades. If not, the troll would have destroyed the table just stopping the conversation.

"Now listen up, both of you!" he ordered, leveling a gnarled finger at us. "I think the current crisis has gone to your heads. You two are overreacting... snapping at shadows! I'll admit we've got some problems, but we've handled worse. This is no time to get panicky."

"But..."

"Hear me out, Aahz. I've listened to you bellow often enough."

I opened my mouth to make a witty comment, then, for once, thought better of it.

"Markie is a potential disaster, but the key word there is *potential*. She's a good kid who will do what we say...*if* we learn to watch what we say to her. The same goes for Bunny. She's smart as a whip and..."

"Bunny?" I blurted, forgetting myself for a moment.

"Yes, Bunny. It's been a long time since there's been anyone around here I could discuss literature and theater with. She's really quite intelligent if you bother to talk to her."

"We *are* talking about the same Bunny, aren't we?" Aahz murmured.

"The one who comes across dumb as a stone," Chumley confirmed grimly. "Just remember how *I* come across when I'm putting on my Big Crunch act...but we're wandering. The subject is problems, and I maintain with a little coaching Bunny won't be one."

He paused to glare at us.

"As to the rumor of Skeeve's abilities at dragon poker, I've never in my life heard anyone get as alarmed as you, Aahz. Sure, there are negative sides to any rumor, but you have to get pretty extreme to do the projections that have been voiced just now."

"Hey, Boss!" Guido called, sticking his head in the door. "The Geek's here to see you."

"I'll handle this," Aahz said, heading for the reception area. "You stay here and listen to what Chumley has to say. He's probably right. I have been edgy lately...for some unknown reason."

"If I am right, then you should hear it, too," the troll called after him.

"Talk to me, Chumley," I said. "That's probably the closest you'll ever hear to an apology from Aahz, anyway."

"Quite right. Where was I? Oh, yes. Even if Aahz's appraisal of the reaction to your success is correct, it shouldn't have too much impact on your work. The small fry may go to other magicians, but you've been trying to cut down on unimportant jobs anyway. When someone is *really* in trouble, they're going to want the best available magician working on it...and right now, that means you."

I thought about what he was saying, weighing it carefully in my mind.

"Even if Aahz is just a little right," I said, "I'm not wild about having any ill feeling generated about me at the Bazaar. Admiration I don't mind, but envy makes me uneasy."

"Now that you'll just have to get used to," the troll laughed, clapping a hand lightly on my shoulder. "Whether you know it or not, that's been building for some time...long before this dragon poker thing came up. You've got a lot going for you, Skeeve, and as long as you do, there will be blokes who envy it."

"So you really think the dragon poker rumors are harmless?"

"Quite right. Really, what harm can come from idle gossip?"

"You know, Chumley, you aren't wrong very often. But when you miss, you really miss."

We looked up to find Aahz leaning in the doorway.

"What's wrong, Aahz? You look like someone just served you water when you were expecting wine."

My partner didn't even smile at my attempted humor.

"Worse than that," he said. "That was the Geek downstairs."

"We know. What did he want?"

"I was hoping he had come to pick up Markie for her father...."

Aahz's voice trailed off to nothing.

"I take it he didn't?" I prompted.

"No, he didn't. In fact, the subject never came up."

Almost without thinking, my partner's hand groped for his oversized goblet of wine.

"He had an invitation...no, make that a challenge. The Sen-Sen Ante Kid has heard about Skeeve here. He wants a showdown match of head-to-head dragon poker. The Geek is making the arrangements."

Chapter X

*"A spoonful of sugar helps the
medicine go down!"*

L. Borgia

JUST LET THE energy flow."

"That's easy for you to say!"

"Did I stutter?"

"You know, Hot Stuff, maybe it would be better
if I..."

"Quit talking and concentrate, Massha."

"You started it."

"And I'm finishing it. Focus on the candle!"

If some of that sounds vaguely familiar, it should.
It's the old 'light the candle' game. Theoretically, it
builds a student's confidence. In actuality, it's a pain in
the butt. Apprentices hate the candle drill. I did when I
was an apprentice. It's a lot more fun when you're on the
teaching end.

"Come on, Skeeve. I'm getting too old to learn this stuff."

"And you're getting older the longer you stall, *apprentice*. Remember, you came to me to learn magic. Just because we've gotten distracted from time to time doesn't mean I've forgotten completely. Now light the candle.

She turned her attention to the exercise again with a mutter I chose to ignore.

I had been thinking hard about my conversations with Aahz and Chumley. The whole question of what to do about the challenge from the Kid was touchy enough that for once I decided to seek the counsel of my advisors before making a commitment I might later regret. Wiser heads than mine were addressing the dilemma at this very moment. Unfortunately, aforesaid wiser heads were in total disagreement as to what course of action to follow.

Aahz was in favor of refusing the match, while Chumley insisted that a refusal would only inflame the situation. He maintained that the only sane way out would be to face the Kid and lose (no one seriously thought I would have a chance in such a game), thereby getting me off the hot seat once and for all. The main problem with that solution was that it involved voluntarily giving up a substantial amount of money...and Aahz wouldn't hear of it.

As the battle raged on, I thought about the earlier portions of our conversations. I thought about parenthood and responsibility. Then I went looking for Massha.

When we first met, Massha was holding down a job as court magician for one of the city-states in the dimension of Jahk...that's right. Where they hold the Big Game every year. The problem was that she didn't really know any magic. She was what is known in the field as a mechanic, and all her powers were purchased across the counter in the form of rings, pendants, and other magical devices. After she saw us strut our stuff in the Big Game, she decided to try to learn some of the non-mechanical variety of magic...and for some unknown reason picked or picked on me to provide her with lessons.

Now, to say the least, I had never thought of Massha as a daughter, but she was my apprentice and therefore a responsibility I had accepted. Unfortunately, I had dodged that responsibility more often than not for the very reasons Aahz had listed: I was unsure of my own abilities and therefore afraid of making a mistake. What I hadn't done was give it my best shot, win or lose. That realization sparked me into a new resolve that if anything happened to Massha in the future, it wouldn't be because I hadn't at least tried to teach her what she asked.

I was also aware that I wanted to learn more about any problems Chumley and Tananda were having, as well as getting a better fix on just who or what Bunny was. At this moment, however, Tananda was absent and Chumley was arguing with Aahz, putting that objective on hold. Bunny was around somewhere, but given a choice between her and Massha, I opted for addressing old obligations before plunging into new ones. Ergo, I rousted out Massha for a long-overdue magic lesson.

"It's just not working, Skeeve. I told you I can't do it."

She sank back in her chair dejected and scowled at the floor. Curious, I reached over and felt the candle wick. It wasn't even warm.

"Not bad," I lied. "You're showing some improvement."

"Don't kid a kidder." Massha grimaced. "I'm not getting anywhere."

"Could you light it with one of your rings?"

She spread her fingers and made a quick inventory.

"Sure. This little trinket right here could do the job, but that's not the point."

"Bear with me. How does it work? Or, more important, how does it feel when it works?"

She gave a quick shrug.

"There's nothing to it. You see, this circle around the stone here moves, and I rotate it according to how tight a beam I want. Pressing the back of the ring activates it, so all I have to do is aim it and relax. The ring does all the work."

"That's it!" I exclaimed, snapping my fingers.

"What's it?"

"Never mind. Keep going. How does it feel?"

"Well," she frowned thoughtfully, "It sort of tingles. It's like I was a hose and there was water rushing through me and out the ring."

"Bingo!"

"What's that supposed to mean?"

"Listen, Massha. Listen closely."

I was speaking carefully now, trying hard to contain my excitement over what I hoped was a major breakthrough.

"Our problem with teaching you non-mechanical magic is that you don't believe in it! I mean, you know that it exists and all, but you don't believe that you can do it. You're working hard at overcoming that every time you try to cast a spell, and that's the problem: You try....You work hard. You know you've got to believe, so you work hard at overcoming your disbelief every time you..."

"Yeah. So?"

"It means you tense up instead of relaxing the way you do when you're working your rings. Tensing blocks the flow of the energies, so you end up with less power at your disposal than you have when you're just walking around. The idea of casting a spell isn't to tense up, it's to relax...if anything, it's an exercise in forced relaxation."

My apprentice bit at her lower lip. "I don't know. That sounds too easy."

"On the one hand it's easy. Viewed a different way, one of the hardest things to do is relax on cue, especially if there's a crisis raging around you at the time."

"So all I have to do is relax?" she asked skeptically.

"Remember that 'hose' feeling you get when you use the ring? That's the energies being channeled through you and focused on your objective. If you pinch off a hose, how much water gets through?"

"I guess that makes sense."

"Try it...now. Reach out your hand and focus on the candle wick as if you were going to use your ring, only don't activate it. Just tell yourself that the ring is working and relax."

She started to say something, then changed her mind. Instead, she drew a deep breath, blew it out, then pointed a finger at the candle.

"Just relax," I urged softly. "Let the energies flow."

"But..."

"Don't talk. Keep your mind on the candle and hear me like I'm talking from a long way off."

Obediently, she focused on the candle.

"Feel the flow of the energies...just like when you're using the ring. Relax some more. Feel how the flow increases? Now, without tensing up, tighten that flow down to a narrow beam and aim it at the wick."

I was concentrating on Massha so much I almost missed it. A small glow of light started to form on the candle wick.

"That's it," I said, fighting to keep my voice calm. "Now..."

"Daddy! Guido says..."

"Ssshh!!!" I hissed. "Not now, Markie! We're trying to light the candle."

She paused in the doorway and cocked her head

85

quizzically.

"Oh, that's easy!" she beamed suddenly and raised her head.

"MARKIE!! DON'T . . ."

But I was too late.

There was a sudden flash of light in the room, and the candle lit. Well, it didn't exactly light, it melted like a bag of water when you take away the bag. So did the candle holder. The table lit, though . . . briefly. At least one corner of it did. It flared for a moment, then the fire died as abruptly as it had appeared. What was left was a charred quarter-circle of tabletop where the corner used to be. That and a table leg standing alone like a burnt-out torch. The fire had hit so fast and smooth the leg didn't even topple over.

I don't remember reaching for Markie, but somehow I had her by the shoulders shaking her.

"WHAT DID YOU DO THAT FOR??" I said in my best paternal tones.

"You . . . you said . . . you wanted the . . . candle lit."

"*That's* lighting a candle?!?"

"I still have a little trouble with control . . . but my teacher says I'm doing better."

I realized I was having a little trouble with control, too. I stopped shaking her and tried to calm myself. This effort was aided by the fact that I noticed that Markie's lip was quivering and she was blinking her eyes rapidly. It suddenly dawned on me that she was about to cry. I decided that, not knowing what would happen when she cried, I would do my best to stay ignorant by heading her off at the pass.

"Umm . . . that was a Fire Elemental, right? Did you learn that at Elemental School?"

Getting someone to talk often serves to stave off tears . . . at least, it had always worked on me.

"Y . . . Yes," she said meekly. "At Elemental School, we learn Fire for starters."

"It's...ummm...very impressive. Look, I'm sorry if I barked at you, Markie, but you see, I didn't just want the candle lit. I wanted Massha to light it. It was part of her magic lesson."

"I didn't know that."

"I know. I didn't think to tell you. That's why I'm apologizing. What happened here was my fault. Okay?"

She nodded her head, exaggerating the motion until it looked like she had a broken neck. It was an interesting illusion, one that I vastly preferred to the idea of her crying...especially in the mood I was in. The thought of Markie with a broken neck...

"Aahh...you *did* interrupt Massha's lesson, though," I said, forcing the other concept from my mind. "Don't you think it would be nice if you apologized to her?"

"That's a great idea, Daddy," she beamed. "I'll do that the next time I see her. Okay?"

That's when I realized my apprentice had slipped out of the room.

* * *

"What do you think you're doing, Massha?"

Leaning casually in the doorway of Massha's bedroom, I realized my voice lacked the intimidating power of Aahz's, but it's the only voice I've got.

"What does it look like I'm doing?" she snarled, carrying a massive armload of clothes from her closet to dump on the bed.

"I'd say, offhand, that it looks like you're packing. The question is, why?"

"People usually pack because it's the easiest way to carry their things when they travel. Less wear and tear on the wardrobe."

Suddenly, I was weary of the banter. Heaving a sigh, I moved in front of her, blocking her path.

"No more games, Massha. Okay? Tell me straight

out, why are you leaving? Don't you owe your teacher that much at least?"

She turned away, busying herself with something on her dresser.

"C'mon, Skeeve," she said in a tone so low I could barely hear it. "You saw what happened downstairs."

"I saw you on the verge of making a major breakthrough in your lessons, if that's what you mean. If Markie hadn't come in, you would have had the candle lit in another few seconds."

"Big deal!"

She spun to face me, and I could see that she was trying not to cry. There seemed to be a lot of that going around.

"Excuse me, Skeeve, but big fat hairy deal. So I can light a candle. So what?! After years of study, Massha can light a candle. . .and a little girl can blow the end off the table without even trying! What does that make me? A magician? Ha ha! What a joke."

"Massha, *I* can't do what Markie did downstairs. . . or what she did in the Bazaar either, for that matter. I told you when you first approached me to be my apprentice exactly how little magic I knew. I'm still learning, though. . .and in the meantime we're still holding our own in the magic business. . .and that's here at the Bazaar. The Magic Capital of the dimensions."

That seemed to settle her a bit, but not much.

"Tell me honestly, Hot Stuff," she said, pursing her lips. "How good do you think I could ever be with magic. . .really?"

"I don't know. I'd like to think that with work and practice you could be better than you are now, though. That's really all any of us can hope for."

"You may be right Skeeve, and it's a good thought. The fact still remains that in the meantime, I'll always be small potatoes around here. . .magically, of course. The way things are going, I'm destined to be a hanger-on. A leech. You and Aahz are nice guys, and you'd never throw me out, but I can't think of one good reason why I should stay."

"I can."

My head came around so fast I was in momentary danger of whiplash. Framed in the doorway was...

"TANANDA!"

"In the flesh," she said with a wink. "But that's not the subject here. Massha, I can't speak for long-term conditions, but I've got one good reason why you shouldn't leave just now. It's the same reason I'm back."

"What's that?"

"It involves the Great Skeeve here. C'mon downstairs. I'm going to brief everybody at once at a war council. We've got a full-blown crisis on our hands."

Chapter XI

"I believe we're under attack."
Col. Travis

ONE OF THE ROOMS in our extra-dimensional palace had a large oval table in it surrounded by chairs. When we moved in, we dubbed it the Conference Room, since there didn't seem to be any other practical use for it. We never used it for conferences, mind you, but it's always nice to have a conference room.

Tonight, however, it was packed to capacity. Apparently Tananda had rounded up the whole household, including Markie and Bunny, before locating Massha and me, and everyone was already seated as we walked in.

"Can we get started now?" Aahz asked caustically. "I *do* have other things to do, you know."

"Really?" Chumley sneered. "Like what?"

"Like talking to the Geek about that invitation," my

partner shot back.

"Without talking to your partner first?"

"I didn't say I was going to refuse or accept. I just want to talk to him about..."

"Can we table the argument for the moment?" I interrupted. "I want to hear what Tananda has to say."

"Thanks, Skeeve," she said, flashing me a quick smile before dropping back into her solemn manner. "I guess you all know I was moving out of here. Well, poking around the Bazaar, I heard a rumor that's changed my mind. If it's true, we're all going to have our hands full dealing with it."

She paused, but no one else said anything. For a change, we were all giving her our undivided attention.

"I guess I should drop the shoe first, then we can all go on from there. The talk on the street is that someone's hired the Ax to do a number on Skeeve."

There was a few heartbeats of silence; then the room exploded.

"Why should anyone..."

"Who's hired the Ax?"

"Where did you hear..."

"Hold it! HOLD IT!" Tananda shouted, holding up her hands for silence. "I can only answer one question at a time...but I'll warn you in advance, I don't have that many answers to start with."

"Who's hired him?" Aahz demanded, seizing first position.

"The way I heard it, a group of magicians here at the Bazaar is none too happy with Skeeve's success. They feel he's taking all the choice assignments these days...getting all the glory work. What they've done is pool their money so they can hire the Ax to do what they're all afraid to do themselves...namely, deal with Skeeve."

"Do you hear that, Chumley? Still think I'm being melodramatic?"

"Shut up, Aahz. Where'd you hear this, little sister?"

"Remember Vic? The little vampire that relocated here from Limbo? Well, he's opened his own magic practice here at the Bazaar. It seems that he was approached to contribute to the fund. He's new enough here that he didn't know any of them by name, but they claim to have the support of nearly a dozen of the smalltime magicians."

"Why didn't he warn us as soon as he heard?"

"He's trying to stay neutral. He didn't contribute, but he also didn't want to be the one to blow the whistle to Skeeve. The only reason he said anything to me was that he was afraid that anyone close to Skeeve might get caught in the crossfire. I must admit, he seems to have a rather exaggerated idea of how much Skeeve here can handle on his own."

"Can I ask a question?" I said grimly. "As the intended victim?"

"Sure, Skeeve. Ask away."

"Who's the Ax?"

At least half the heads at the table swiveled toward me while the faces attached to them dropped their jaws.

"You're kidding!"

"Don't you know who..."

"Aahz, didn't you teach him any..."

"Whoa! Hold it! I shouted over the clamor. "I can only take so much of this informative babbling at one time. Aahz! As my friend, partner, and sometimes mentor, could you deign to tell me in simple terms who the Ax is?"

"Nobody knows."

I closed my eyes and gave my head a small shake in an effort to clear my ears. After all this "Gee, why don't you know that?" brouhaha, I could swear he said...

"He's right, handsome," Tananda chimed in. "The Ax's real identity is one of the most closely guarded secrets in all the dimensions. That's why he's so effective at what he does."

"That may be true," I nodded. "But from the reaction in this room when you dropped the name, I'd guess that somebody knows *something* about him. Now, let me rephrase the question. If you don't know *who* the Ax is, could someone enlighten me as to *what* he is?"

"The Ax is the greatest Character Assassin in all the dimensions," Aahz said with a snarl. "He works freelance and charges fees that make ours look like pocket change. Once the Ax is on your tail, though, you might as well kiss it goodbye. He's ruined more careers than five stock-market crashes. Haven't you ever heard the expression 'take the ax to someone'? Well, that's where it comes from."

I felt that all-too-familiar "down elevator" sensation in my stomach.

"How does he do it?"

"It varies," my partner shrugged. "He tailor-makes his attack depending on the assignment. The only constant is that whatever you were when he started, you're not when he's done."

"I wish you'd quit saying 'you' all the time. I'm not dead yet."

"Sorry, partner. Figure of speech."

"Well, that's just swell!" Guido exploded. "How're Nunzio n' me supposed to guard the Boss when we don't know what's comin' at him?"

"You don't," Aahz shot back. "This is out of your category, Guido. We're talking about character assassination, not a physical attack. It's not in your job description."

"Izzat so!" Nunzio said in his squeaky voice. "Don Bruce says we should guard him. I don't remember him sayin' anything about physical or non-physical attacks. Right, Guido?"

"That's right! If the Boss has got someone after his

scalp, guardin' him is our job...if that's all right with you, MISTER Aahz!"

"I wouldn't trust you two to guard a fish head, much less my partner!" Aahz roared, surging to his feet.

"Stop it, Aahz!" Tananda ordered, kicking my partner's chair so that it cut his legs out from under him and plopped him back into his seat. "If we're up against the Ax, we're going to need all the help we can get. Let's stop bickering about the 'who' and concentrate on the 'how.' Okay? We're all scared, but that doesn't mean we should turn on each other when it's the Ax that's our target."

That cooled everybody down for the moment. There were a few glares and mutters exchanged, but at least the volume level dropped to where I could be heard.

"I think you're all overlooking something," I said quietly.

"What's that?" Tananda blinked.

"Aahz came close a minute ago. This is my problem...and it's not really in any of your job descriptions. We're all friends, and there are business ties between Aahz and me, as well as Guido and Nunzio, but we're talking about reputations here. If I get hit, and everyone seems to be betting against me right now, anyone standing close to me is going to get mud splashed on them, too. It seems to me that the best course of action is for the rest of you to pull back, or, better still, for me to move out and present a solo target. That way, we're only running the risk of having one career ruined...mine. I got where I am by standing on your shoulders. If I can't maintain it on my own, well, maybe it wasn't much of a career to start with."

The whole room was staring at me as I lurched to a halt.

"You know, Skeeve old boy," Chumley said, clearing his throat, "As much as I like you, some times it's difficult to remember just how intelligent you are."

"I'll say," Tananda snarled. "That's about the dumbest...Wait a minute! Does this have anything to do with my leaving?"

"A bit," I admitted. "And Massha leaving and Aahz's talking about responsibility, and..."

"Stop right there!" Aahz ordered, holding up his hand. "Let's talk about responsibility, *partner*. It's funny that *I* should have to lecture *you* about this, but there are all sorts of responsibilities. One of the ones that I've learned about from you is the responsibility to one's friends: helping them out when they're in trouble, *and* letting them help you in return. I haven't forgotten how you came into a strange dimension to bust me out of prison after I'd refused your help in the first place; or how you signed us on to play in the Big Game to bail Tananda out after she was caught thieving; or how you insisted that Don Bruce assign Guido and Nunzio here to you when they were in line for disciplinary action after botching their assignment for the Mob. I haven't forgotten it, and I'll bet they haven't either, even if you have. Now, I suggest you shut up about job descriptions and let your friends help you...*partner*."

"A-bloody-men." Chumley nodded.

"You could have left me with the Geek for the slavers," Markie said thoughtfully, in a surprisingly adult voice.

"So, now that that's settled," my partner said, rubbing his hands together, "let's get to work. My buddy Guido here has raised a good point. How do we defend Skeeve when we don't know how or when the Ax will strike?"

We hadn't really settled it, and Aahz wasn't about to give me a chance to point it out. I was just as glad, though, since I really didn't know what to say.

"All we can do is be on the lookout for anyone or anything strange showing up." Tananda shrugged.

"Like a showdown match of dragon poker with the Sen-Sen Ante Kid," Chumley said, staring into the distance.

"What's that?"

"You missed it, little sister. It seems that our boy Skeeve has drawn the attention of the king of dragon poker. He wants a head-to-head showdown match, and he wants it soon."

"Don't look at me like that, Chumley." Aahz grimaced. "I'm changing my vote. If we want to preserve Skeeve's reputation, there's no way he can refuse the challenge. *Now* I'm willing to admit it'll be money well spent."

"My daddy can beat anybody at dragon poker," Markie declared loyally.

"Your daddy can get his brains beaten out royally," my partner corrected gently. "I just hope we can teach him enough between now and game time that he can lose gracefully."

"I don't like it," Tananda growled. "It's too convenient. Somehow this game has the Ax's fingerprints all over it."

"You're probably right," Aahz sighed. "But there's not much else we can do except accept the challenge and try to make the best of a bad situation."

"Bite the bullet and play the cards we're dealt. Eh, Aahz?" I murmured.

I thought I had spoken quietly, but everyone around the table winced, including Markie. They might be loyal enough to risk their lives and careers defending me, but they weren't going to laugh at my jokes.

"Wait a minute!" Nunzio squeaked. "Do you think there's a chance that the Kid is actually the Ax?"

"Low probability," Bunny said, speaking for the first time in the meeting. "Someone like the Ax has to work a low profile. The Sen-Sen Ante Kid is too noticeable. If he were a character assassin, people would

97

notice in no time flat. Besides, when he wins, nobody thinks it's because his opponents are disreputable. . .it's because the Kid is good. No, I figure the Ax has got to be like the purloined letter. . .he can hide in plain sight. Figure the last person you'd suspect, and you'll be getting close to his real identity."

The conversation swirled on around me, but I didn't listen very closely. For some reason, a thought had occurred to me while Bunny was talking. We had all been referring to the Ax as a "he," but if no one knew his real identity, he could just as easily be a "she." If anything, men were much less defensive and more inclined to brag about the details of their careers when they were with a woman.

Bunny was a woman. She had also appeared suddenly on our doorstep right around the time the Ax was supposed to be getting his assignment. We already knew that she was smarter than she let on. . .words like "purloined" didn't go with the vacant stare she so carefully cultivated. What better place for the Ax to strike from than the inside?

I decided that I should have a little chat with my moll as soon as the opportunity presented itself.

Chapter XII

"No one should hide their true self
behind a false face."
L. Chaney

IT WAS WITH a certain amount of trepidation that I approached Bunny's bedroom. In case you haven't noticed, my experience with women is rather limited... like to the fingers of one hand limited.

Tananda, Massha, Luanna, Queen Hemlock, and now Bunny were the only adult females I had ever had to deal with, and thus far my track record was less than glowing. I had had a crush on Tananda for a while, but now she was more of a big sister to me. Massha was...well, Massha. I guess if anything I saw her as a kid sister, someone to be protected and sometimes cuddled. I've never really understood her open admiration of me, but it had stood firm through some of my most embarrassing mishaps and made it easy for me to confide in her. Even though I still thought of Luanna as my one true love, I had only spoken to her on four occasions, and after our last exchange I wasn't sure there would ever be a fifth meeting. The only relationship I had had with a woman which was more disastrous than my attempt at love was the one I had had with Queen Hemlock. She might not shoot me on sight, but there was no doubt in anyone's mind that she would like to...and she's the one who wanted to marry me!

Of course, none of the women I had dealt with so far was anything like Bunny, though whether this was good or bad I wasn't entirely sure. The fact still remained, however, that I was going to have to learn more about her, for two reasons: first, if she was going to be a resident of our household, I wanted to get a better fix on where she was coming from so I could treat her as something other than a mad aunt in the cellar; and second, if she was the Ax, the sooner I found out, the better. Unfortunately, the only way I could think of to obtain the necessary information was to talk to her.

I raised my hand, hesitated for a moment, then rapped on her door. It occurred to me that, even though I had never been in front of a firing squad, now I knew how it felt.

"Who is it?"

"It's Skeeve, Bunny. Have you got a minute?"

The door flew open and Bunny was there, grabbing my arm and pulling me inside. She was dressed in a slinky jumpsuit with the neck unlaced past her navel, which was a great relief to me. When I called on Queen Hemlock in her bedroom, she had received me in the altogether.

"Geez! It's good to see you. I was startin' to think you weren't ever comin' by!"

With a double-jointed shift of her hips she bumped the door shut, while her hands flew to the lacings in her outfit. So much for being relieved.

"If you just give me a second, hon, I'll be all set to go. You kinda caught me unprepared, and..."

"Bunny, could you just knock it off for a while? Huh?"

For some reason the events of the last few days suddenly rested heavy on my shoulders, and I just wasn't in the mood for games.

She stared at me with eyes as big as a Pervect's bar bill, but her hands ceased their activity. "What's the matter, Skeevie? Don't you like me?"

"I really don't know, Bunny," I said heavily. "You've never really given me a chance, have you?"

She drew in a sharp breath and started to retort angrily. Then she hesitated and looked away suddenly, licking her lips nervously.

"I...I don't know what you mean. Didn't I come to your room and try to be friendly?"

"I think you *do* know what I mean," I pressed, sensing a weakening in her defenses. "Every time we see each other, you're hitting me in the face with your 'sex-kitten' routine. I never know whether to run or applaud, but neither action is particularly conducive to getting to know you."

"Don't knock it," she said. "It's a great little bit. It's gotten me this far, hasn't it? Besides, isn't that what men want from a girl?"

"I don't."

"Really?"

There was a none-too-gentle mockery in her voice. She took a deep breath and pulled her shoulders back. "So tell me, what *does* cross your mind when I do this?"

Regardless of what impression I may have left on you from my earlier exploits, I do think fast. Fast enough to censor my first three thoughts before answering.

"Mostly discomfort," I said truthfully. "It's impressive, all right, but I get the feeling I should do something about it and I'm not sure I'm up to it."

She smiled triumphantly and let her breath out, easing the tension across her chest and my mind. Of the two, I think my mind needed it more.

"You have just hit on the secret of the sex kittens. It's not that you don't like it. There's just too much of it for you to be sure you can handle it. '

"I'm not sure I follow you."

"Men like to brag and strut a lot, but they've got egos as brittle as spun glass. If a girl calls their bluff, comes at them like a seething volcano that can't be put out, men get scared. Instead of fanning a gentle feminine ember, they're faced with a forest fire, so they take their wind elsewhere. Oh, they keep us around to impress people. 'Look at the tigress I've tamed,' and all that. But when we're alone they usually keep their distance. I'll bet a moll sees less actual action than your average coed...except our pay scale is a lot better."

That made me think. On the one hand, she had called my reaction pretty close. Her roaring come-on *had* scared me a bit...well, a lot. Still, there was the other hand.

"It sounds like you don't think very much of men," I observed.

"Hey! Don't get me wrong. They're a lot better than the alternatives. I just got a little sick of listening to the same old lines over and over and decided to turn the tables on 'em. That's all."

"That wasn't what I meant. A second ago you said 'That's what men want from a girl.' It may be true, and I won't try to argue the point. It's uncomfortably close to 'That's *all* men want from a girl,' though, and that I *will* argue."

She scowled thoughtfully and chewed her lower lip. "I guess that *is* over-generalizing a bit," she admitted.

"Good."

"It's more accurate to say 'That's all men want from a *beautiful* girl.'"

"Bunny..."

"No, you listen to me, Skeeve. This is one subject I've had a lot more experience at than you have. It's fine to talk about minds when you look like Massha. But when you grow up looking good like I did—no brag, just a statement of fact—it's one long string of men hitting on you. If they're interested in your mind, I'd say they need a crash course in anatomy!"

In the course of our friendship, I had had many long chats with Massha about what it meant to a woman to be less than attractive. However, this was the first time I had ever been made to realize that beauty might be something less than an asset.

"I don't recall 'hitting on you,' Bunny."

"Okay, okay. Maybe I *have* taken to counter-punching before someone else starts. There's been enough of a pattern that I think I'm justified in jumping to conclusions. As I recall, you were a little preoccupied when we met. How would you have reacted if we ran into each other casually in a bar?"

That wasn't difficult at all to imagine... unfortunately.

"Touche!" I acknowledged. "Let me just toss one thought at you, Bunny. Then I'll yield to your experience. The question of sex is going to hang in the air over *any* male-female encounter until it's resolved. I think it lingers from pre-civilization days when survival of the species hinged on propagation. It's strongest when encountering a member of the opposite sex one finds attractive...such as a beautiful woman, or, I believe the phrase is, a 'hunk.' Part of civilization, though I don't know how many other people think of it this way, is setting rules and laws to help settle that question quickly: siblings, parents, and people under age or married to someone else are off limits...well, usually, but you get my point. Theoretically, this allows people to spend less time sniffing at each other and more time getting on with other endeavors...like art or business. I'm not sure it's an improvement, mind you, but it has brought us a long way."

"That's an interesting theory, Skeeve," Bunny said thoughtfully. "Where'd you hear it?"

"I made it up," I admitted.

"I'll have to mull that one over for a while. Even if you're right, though, what does it prove?"

"Well, I guess I'm trying to say that I think you're focusing too much on the existence of the question. Each time it comes up, resolve it and move on to other things. Specifically, I think we can resolve the question between us right now. As far as I'm concerned, the answer is no, or at least not for a long time. If we can agree on that, I'd like to move on to other things...like getting to know you better."

"I'd say that sounds like a pass, if you weren't saying 'no' in the same breath. Maybe I have been a little hypersensitive on the subject. Okay. Agreed. Let's try it as friends."

She stuck out her hand, and I shook it solemnly. In the back of my mind was a twinge of guilt. Now that I had gotten her to relax her guard, I was going to try to pump her for information.

"What would you like to know?"

"Well, except for the fact that you're smarter than you let on and that you're Don Bruce's niece, I really don't know much about you at all!"

"Whoops," she giggled, "You weren't even supposed to know about the niece part."

It was a much nicer giggle than her usual brain-jarring squeal.

"Let's start there, then. I understand your uncle doesn't approve of your career choice."

"You can say that again. He had a profession all picked out for me, put me through school and everything. The trouble was that he didn't bother to check with me.

Frankly, I'd rather do anything else than what he had in mind."

"What was that?"

"He wanted me to be an accountant."

My mind flashed back to my old nemesis J. R. Grimble back at Possletum. Trying to picture Bunny in his place was more than my imagination could manage.

"Umm...I suppose accounting is okay work. I can see why Don Bruce didn't want you to follow his footsteps into a life of crime."

Bunny cocked a skeptical eyebrow at me. "If you believe that, you don't know much about accounting."

"Whatever. It does occur to me that there are more choices for one's livelihood than being an accountant or being a moll."

"I don't want to set you off again," she smirked, "but my looks were working against me. Most legitimate businessmen were afraid that if they hired me their wives, or partners, or board of directors, or staff would think they were putting a mistress on the payroll. After a while I decided to go with the flow and go into a field where being attractive was a requirement instead of a handicap. If I'm guilty of anything, it's laziness."

"I don't know," I said, shaking my head. "I'll admit I don't think much of your career choice."

"Oh, yeah? Well, before you start sitting in moral judgment, let me tell you..."

"Whoa! Time out!" I interrupted. "What I meant was there isn't much of a future in it. Nothing personal, but nobody stays young and good-looking forever. From what I hear, your job doesn't have much of a retirement plan."

"None of the Mob jobs do," she shrugged. "It pays the bills while I'm looking for something better."

Now we were getting somewhere.

"Speaking of the Mob, Bunny, I'll admit this Ax thing has me worried. Do you know offhand if the Mob ever handles character assassination? Maybe I could talk to someone and get some advice."

"I don't think they do. It's a little subtle for them. Still, I've never known Uncle Bruce to turn down any kind of work if the profit was high enough."

It occurred to me that that was a fairly evasive no-answer. I decided to try again.

"Speaking of your uncle, do you have any idea why he picked you for this assignment?"

There was the barest pause before she answered.

"No. I don't."

I had survived the Geek's dragon poker game watching other people, and I'm fairly good at it. To me, that hesitation was a dead giveaway. Bunny knew why she was here, she just wasn't telling.

As if she had read my thoughts, a startled look came over her face.

"Hey! It just dawned on me. Do you think I'm the Ax? Believe me, Skeeve, I'm not. Really!"

She was very sincere and very believable. Of course, if I were the Ax, that's exactly what I would say and how I would say it.

Chapter XIII

"Your Majesty should pay attention
to his appearance."
H. C. Anderson

THERE ARE many words to describe the next day's outing into the Bazaar. Unfortunately, none of them are "calm," "quiet," or "relaxing." Words like "zoo," "circus," and "chaos" spring much more readily to mind.

It started before we even left our base...specifically, over whether or not we should go out at all.

Aahz and Massha maintained that we should go to ground until things blew over, on the theory that it would provide the fewest opportunities for the Ax to attack. Guido and Nunzio sided with them, adding their own colorful phrases to the proceedings. "Going to the mattresses" was one of their favorites, an expression which never ceased to conjure intriguing images to my

107

mind. Like I told Bunny, I'm not *totally* pure.

Tananda and Chumley took the other side, arguing that the best defense is a solid offense. Staying inside, they argued, would only make us sitting ducks. The only sane thing to do would be to get out and try to determine just what the Ax was going to try. Markie and Bunny chimed in supporting the brother-sister team, though I suspect it was more from a desire to see more of the Bazaar.

After staying neutral and listening for over an hour while the two sides went at each other, I finally cast my vote...in favor of going out. Strangely enough, my reasons aligned most closely with those of Bunny and Markie: while I was more than a little afraid of going out and being a moving target, I was even more afraid of being cooped up inside with my own team while they got progressively more nervous and short-tempered with each other.

No sooner was that resolved than a new argument erupted, this time over who was going along. Obviously, everyone wanted to go. Just as obviously, if everybody did, we would look like exactly what we were: a strike force looking for trouble. I somehow didn't think this would assist our efforts to preserve my reputation.

After another hour of name-calling, we came up with a compromise. We would all go. For discretion as well as strategic advantage, however, it was decided that part of the team would go in disguise. That is, in addition to making our party look smaller than it really was, it would also allow our teammates to watch from a short distance and, more important, listen to what was being said around us in the Bazaar. Aahz, Tananda, Chumley, Massha, and Nunzio would serve as our scouts and reserve, while Markie, Bunny, Guido, and I would act as the bait...a role I liked less the more I thought about it.

Thus it was that we finally set out on our morning

stroll...early in the afternoon.

On the surface the Bazaar was unchanged, but it didn't take long before I began to notice some subtle differences. I had gotten so used to maintaining disguise spells that I could keep our five colleagues incognito without it eating into my concentration...which was just as well, because there was a lot to concentrate on.

Apparently word of our last shopping venture had spread, and the reaction among the Deveel merchants to our appearance in the stalls was mixed and extreme. Some of the displays closed abruptly as we approached, while others rushed to meet us. There were, of course, those who took a neutral stance, neither closing nor meeting us halfway, but rather watching us carefully as we looked over their wares. Wherever we went, however, I noticed a distinct lack of enthusiasm for the favorite Bazaar pastime of haggling. Prices were either declared firm or counteroffers stacked up with minimum verbiage. It seems that, while they still wanted our money, the Deveels weren't eager to prolong contact with us.

I wasn't sure exactly how to handle the situation. I could take advantage of their nervousness and drive some shameless bargains, or grit my teeth and pay more than I thought the items were worth. The trouble was that neither course would do much to improve my image in the eyes of the merchants or erase the memory of our last outing.

Of course, my life being what it is, there were distractions.

After our talk, Bunny had decided that we were friends and attacked her new role with the same enthusiasm she brought to playing a vamp. She still clung to my arm, mind you, and from a distance probably still looked like a moll. Her attention, however, was now centered on me instead of on herself.

Today she had decided to voice her opinion of my wardrobe.

"Really, Skeeve. We've *got* to get you some decent clothes."

She had somehow managed to get rid of her nasal voice as well as whatever it was she had always been chewing on. Maybe there was a connection there.

"What's wrong with what I'm wearing?"

I had on what I considered to be one of my spiffier outfits. The stripes on the pants were two inches wide and alternated yellow and light green, while the tunic was a brilliant red and purple paisley number.

"I wouldn't know where to start," she said, wrinkling her nose. "Let's just say it's a bit on the garish side."

"You didn't say anything about my clothes before."

"Right. Before. As in 'before we decided to be friends.' Molls don't stay employed by telling their men how tacky they dress. Sometimes I think one of the qualifications for having a decorative lady on your arm is to have no or negative clothes sense."

"Of course, I don't have much firsthand knowledge, but aren't there a few molls who dress a little flamboyantly themselves?" I said archly.

"True. But I'll bet if you checked into it, they're wearing outfits their men bought for them to dress up in. When we went shopping, you let me do the selecting and just picked up the bill. A lot of men figure if they're paying the fare, they should have the final say as to what their baby-doll wears. Let's face it, molls have to pay attention to how they look because their jobs depend on it. A girl who dresses like a sack of potatoes doesn't find work as a moll."

"So you're saying I dress like a sack of potatoes?"

"If a sack looked like you, it would knock the eyes out of the potatoes."

I groaned my appreciation. Heck, if no one was going to laugh at my jokes, why should I laugh at theirs? Of course, I filed her comment away for future use if the

110

occasion should arise.

"Seriously though, Skeeve, your problem is that you dress like a kid. You've got some nice pieces in your wardrobe, but nobody's bothered to show you how to wear them. Bright outfits are nice, but you've got to balance them. Wearing a pattern with a muted solid accents the pattern. Wearing a pattern with a pattern is trouble, unless you really know what you're doing. More often than not, the patterns end up fighting each other...and if they're in two different colors you've got an all-out war. Your clothes should call attention to you, not to themselves."

Despite my indignation, I found myself being drawn into what she was saying. If there's one thing I've learned in my various adventures, it's that you take information where you find it.

"Let's see if I'm following you, Bunny. What you're saying is that just buying nice items, especially ones that catch my eye, isn't enough. I've got to watch how they go together...try to build a coordinated total. Right?"

"That's part of it," she nodded. "But I think we'd better go back to step one for a moment if we're going to educate you right. First, you've got to decide on the image you want to project. Your clothes make a statement about you, but you've got to know what that statement should be. Now, bankers depend on people trusting them with their money, so they dress conservatively to give the impression of dependability. No one will give their money to a banker who looks like he spends his afternoons playing the ponies. At the other end of the scale, you have the professional entertainers. They make their money getting people to look at them, so their outfits are usually flashy and flamboyant."

This was fascinating. Bunny wasn't telling me a thing I hadn't seen for myself, but she was defining patterns that hadn't registered on me before. Suddenly the whole clothes thing was starting to make sense.

"So what kind of image do I project?"

"Well, since you ask, right now you look like one of two things: either someone who's so rich and successful that he doesn't have to care what other people think, or like a kid who doesn't know how to dress. Here at the Bazaar, they know you're successful, so the merchants jump to the first conclusion and drag out every gaudy item they haven't been able to unload on anyone else and figure if they price it high enough, you'll go for it."

"A sucker or a fool," I murmured. "I don't really know what image I want, but it isn't either of those."

"Try this one on for size. You're a magician for hire, right? You want to look well off so your clients know you're good at what you do, but not so rich that they'll think you're overcharging them. You don't want to go too conservative, because in part they're buying into the mystique of magic, but if you go too flashy you'll look like a sideshow charlatan. In short, I think your best bet is to try for 'quiet power.' Someone who is apart from the workaday crowd, but who is so sure of himself that he doesn't have to openly try for attention."

"How do I look like that?"

"That's where Bunny comes in," she said with a wink. "If we're agreed on the end, I'll find the means. Follow me."

With that, she led me off into one of the most incredible shopping sprees I've ever taken part in. She insisted that I change into the first outfit we bought: a light blue open-necked shirt with cream-colored slacks and a matching neck scarf. Markie protested that she had liked the pretty clothes better, but as we made our way from stall to stall, I noticed a change in the manner of the proprietors. They still seemed a little nervous about our presence, but they were bringing out a completely different array of clothes for our examination, and several of them complimented me on what I was wearing...something that had never happened before.

I must admit I was a little surprised at how much some of these "simple and quiet" items cost, but Bunny assured me that the fabric and the workmanship justified the price.

"I don't understand it," I quipped at one point. "I thought that accountants were all tightfisted, and here you are: the ultimate consumer."

"You don't see me reaching for *my* bankroll, do you?" she purred back. "Accountants can deal with necessary expenses, as long as it's someone else's money. Our main job is to get you maximum purchase power for your hard-earned cash."

And so it went. When I had time to think, it occurred to me that if Bunny *was* the Ax, she was working awfully hard to make me look good. I was still trying to figure out how this could fit into a diabolical plan when I felt a nudge at my elbow. Glancing around, I found Aahz standing next to me.

Now, when I throw my disguise spell, I still see the person as they normally are. That's why I started nervously before I remembered that to anyone else at the Bazaar he looked like a fellow shopper exchanging a few words.

"Nice outfit, partner," he said. "It looks like your little playmate is doing some serious work on your wardrobe."

"Thanks, Aahz. Do you really like it?"

"Sure. There *is* one little item you might add to your list before we head for home."

"What's that?"

"About five decks of cards. While he might be impressed by your new image, I think it'll make a bigger impact on the Kid if you spend a little time learning how to play dragon poker before you square off with him."

That popped my bubble in a hurry. Aahz was right.

113

Clothes and the Ax aside, there was one thing I was going to have to face up to soon, and that was a showdown with the best dragon poker player in all the dimensions.

Chapter XIV

"Sometimes luck isn't enough."
L. Luciano

OGRE'S HIGH, Skeeve. Your bet."

"Oh! Umm...I'll go ten."

"Bump you ten."

"Out."

"Twenty to me? I'll go twenty on top of that."

"Call."

By now, you should know that sound. That's right. Dragon poker in full gallop. This time, however, it was a friendly game between Aahz, Tananda, Chumley, and me. Of course, I'm using the phrase "friendly" rather loosely here.

Aside from occasional shouting matches, I had never been in a fight with these three before. That is, when there had been trouble, we formed our circle with the horns out, not in. For the first time I found myself on

115

the opposite side of a conflict from my colleagues, and I wasn't enjoying it at all. Realizing this was just a game, and a practice game at that, I was suddenly very glad I didn't have to face any one of them in a real life-and-death situation.

The banter was still there, but there was an edge on it. There was a cloud of tension over the table as the players focused on each other like circling predators. It had been there at the game at the Even-Odds, but then I was expecting it. One doesn't expect support or sympathy from total strangers in a card game. The trouble was that these three who were my closest friends were turning out to be total strangers when the chips were down... if you'll pardon the expression.

"I think you're bluffing, big brother. Up another forty."

I gulped and pushed another stack of my diminishing pile of chips into the pot.

"Call."

"You got me," the troll shrugged. "Out."

"Well, Skeeve. That leaves you and me. I've got an elf-high flush."

She displayed her hand and looked at me expectantly. I turned my hole cards over with what I hoped was a confident flourish.

Silence reigned as everyone bent forward to stare at my hand.

"Skeeve, this is garbage," Tananda said at last. "Aahz folded a better hand than this without his hole cards. I had you beat on the board."

"What she's trying to say, partner," Aahz smirked, "is that you should have either folded or raised. Calling the bet when the cards she has showing beat your hand is just tossing away money."

"Okay, okay! I get the point."

"Do you? You've still got about fifty chips there. Are you sure you don't want to wait until you've lost those, too? Or maybe we should redivide the chips and start over... *again.*"

"Lighten up, Aahz," Tananda ordered. "Skeeve had a system that had worked for him before. Why shouldn't he want to try it out before being forcefed something new?"

What they were referring to was my original resistance to taking lessons in dragon poker. I had pretty much decided to handle the upcoming game the same way I had played the game at the Even-Odds rather than try to crash-learn the rules. After some discussion (read: argument) it was agreed that we should play a demonstration game so that I could show my coaches how well my system worked.

Well, I showed them.

I could read Aahz pretty well, possibly because I knew him so intimately. Chumley and Tananda, though, threw me for a loop. I was unable to pick up any sort of giveaway clues in their speech or manner, nor could I manage to detect any apparent relationship between their betting and what they were holding. In a depressingly short period of time I had been cleaned out of my starting allotment of chips. Then we divvied the stacks up again and started over... with the same results. We were now closing in on the end of the third round, and I was ready to throw in the towel.

As much as I would have liked to tell myself that I was having a bad run of cards or that we had played too few hands to set the patterns, the horrible truth was that I was simply outclassed. I mean, usually I could spot if a player had a good hand. Then the question was "how good," or more specifically, if his was better than mine. Of course, the same went for weak hands. I depended on being able to detect a player who was betting a hand that needed development or if he was simply betting that the other hand in the round would develop worse than his. In this "demonstration game," however, I was caught flatfooted again and again. Too many times a hand that I had figured for guts-nothing turned out to be a powerhouse.

To say the least, it was depressing. These were players who wouldn't dream of challenging the Sen-Sen Ante Kid themselves, and they were cleaning my clock without half trying.

"I know when I'm licked, Aahz," I said. "Even if it does take me a little longer than most. I'm ready to take those lessons you offered...if you still think it will do any good."

"Sure it will, partner. At the very least, I don't think it can hurt your game, if tonight's been an accurate sample."

Trust a Pervect to know just what to say to cheer you up.

"Come on, Aahz old boy," Chumley interrupted. "Skeeve here is doing the best he can. He's just trying to hang on in a bad situation...like we all do. Let's not make it any rougher for him. Hmmm?"

"I suppose you're right."

"And watch comments like that when Markie's around," Tananda put in. "She's got a bad case of hero-worship for her new daddy, and we need him as an authority figure to keep her in line."

"Speaking of Markie," my partner grimaced, peering around, "where is our portable disaster area?"

The tail end of our shopping expedition had not gone well. Markie's mood seemed to deteriorate as the day wore on. Twice we were saved from total disaster only by timely intervention by our spotters when she started to get particularly upset. Not wishing to push our luck, I called a halt to the excursion, which almost triggered another tantrum from my young ward. I wondered if other parents had ever had shopping trips cut short by a cranky child.

"She's off somewhere with Bunny and the bodyguards. I thought this session would be rough enough without the added distraction of Markie cheering for her daddy."

"Good call," Chumley said. "Well, enough chitchat. Shall we have at it?"

"Right!" Aahz declared, rubbing his hands together as he leaned forward. "Now, the first thing we have to do is tighten up your betting strategy. If you keep..."

"Umm...Aren't you getting a little ahead of yourself, Aahz?" Tananda interrupted.

"How so?"

"Don't you think it would be nice if we taught him the sequence of hands first? It's a lot easier to bet when you know whether or not your hand is any good."

"Oh. Yeah. Of course."

"Let me handle this part, Aahz," the troll volunteered. "Now then, Skeeve. The ascending sequence of hands is as follows:

High Card
One Pair
Two Pair
Three Of A Kind
Three Pair
Full House (Three Of A Kind plus a Pair)
Four Of A Kind
Flush
Straight (those last two are ranked higher and reversed because of the sixth card)
Full Belly (two sets of Three Of A Kind)
Full Dragon (Four Of a Kind plus a Pair)
Straight Flush
Have you got that?"

Half an hour later, I could almost get through the list without referring to my crib sheet. By that time, my teachers' enthusiasm was noticeably dimmed. I decided to push on to the next lesson before I lost them completely.

"Close enough," I declared. "I can bone up on these on my own time. Where do we go from here? How much should I bet on which hands?"

"Not so fast," Aahz said. "First, you've got to finish learning about the hands."

"You mean there are more? I thought..."

"No. You've got all the hands...or will have, with a little practice. Now you've got to learn about *conditional modifiers.*"

"Conditional modifiers?" I echoed weakly.

"Sure. Without 'em, dragon poker would be just another straightforward game. Are you starting to see why I didn't want to take the time before to teach you?"

I nodded silently, staring at my list of card hands that I somehow had a feeling was about to become more complex.

"Cheer up, Skeeve," Chumley said gaily, clapping me on the shoulder. "This is going to be easier than if we were trying to teach you the whole game."

"It is?" I blinked, perking up slightly.

"Sure. You see, the conditional modifiers depend on certain variables, like the day of the week, the number of players, chair position, things like that. Now since this match is prearranged, we know what most of those variables will be. For example, there will only be the two of you playing, and as the challenged party you have your choice of chairs...pick the one facing south, incidentally."

"What my big brother is trying to say in his own clumsy way," Tananda interrupted by squeezing my arm softly, "is that you don't have to learn *all* the conditional modifiers. Just the ones that will be in effect for your game with the Kid."

"Oh. I get it. Thanks, Chumley. That makes me feel a lot better."

"Right-o. There can't be more than a dozen or two that will be pertinent."

The relief I had been feeling turned cold inside me. "Two dozen conditional modifiers?"

"C'mon, big brother. There aren't that many."

"I was going to say I thought he was underestimating," Aahz grinned.

"Well, let's bloody well count them off and see."

"Red dragons will be wild on even-numbered hands...."

"...But unicorns will be wild all evening...."

"...The corps-a-corps hand will be invalid all night, that's why we didn't bother to list it, partner...."

"...Once a night, a player can change the suit of one of his up cards...."

"...Every five hands, the sequence of cards is reversed, so the low cards are high and vice versa...."

"...Threes will be dead all night and treated as blank cards...."

"...And once a four-of-a-kind is played, that card value is also dead...."

"...Unless it's a wild card, then it simply ceases to be wild and can be played normally...."

"...If there's a ten showing in the first two face-up cards in each hand, then sevens will be dead...."

"...Unless there is a second ten showing, then it cancels the first...."

"...Of course, if the first card turned face up in a round is an Ogre, the round will be played with an extra hole card, four face up and five face down...."

"...A natural hand beats a hand of equal value built with wild cards...."

"Hey—that's not a conditional modifier. That's a regular rule."

"It will still be in effect, won't it? Some of the conditional modifiers nullify standing rules, so I thought we should..."

"ARE YOU PUTTING ME ON?!!"

The conversation stopped on a dime as my coaches

turned to stare at me.

"I mean, this is a joke. Right?"

"No, partner," Aahz said carefully. "This is what dragon poker is all about. Like Chumley said, just be thankful you're only playing one night and get to learn the abbreviated list."

"But how am I supposed to stand a chance in this game? I'm not even going to be able to remember all the rules."

An awkward silence came over the table.

"I...uhh...think you've missed the point, Skeeve," Tananda said at last. "You don't stand a chance. The Kid is the best there is. There's no way you can learn enough in a few days or a few years to even give him a run for his money. All we're trying to do is teach you enough so that you won't embarrass yourself—as in ruin the reputation of the Great Skeeve—while he whittles away at your stake. You've got to at least *look* like you know what you're doing. Otherwise you come across as a fool who doesn't know enough to know how little he knows."

I thought about that for a few.

"Doesn't that description actually fit me to a 'T'?"

"If so, let's keep it in the family. Okay?" my partner winked, punching me playfully on the shoulder. "Cheer up, Skeeve. In some ways it should be fun. There's nothing like competing in a game without the pressure to win to let you role-play to the hilt."

"Sure, Aahz."

"Okay, so let's get back to it. Just listen this time around. We'll go over it again slower later so you can write it all down."

With that, they launched into it again.

I listened with half an ear, all the while examining my feelings. I had gone into the first game at the Even-Odds expecting to lose, but I had been viewing that as a social evening. It was beyond my abilities to kid myself into believing this match with the Kid was going to be social. As much as I respected the views of my advisors, I was having a lot of trouble accepting the idea that I would help my reputation by losing. They were right, though, that I couldn't gracefully refuse the challenge. If I didn't stand a chance of winning, then the only option left was to lose gracefully. Right?

Try as I might, though, I couldn't still a little voice in the back of my mind that kept telling me that the ideal solution would be to take the Kid to the cleaners. Of course, that was impossible. Right? Right?

Chapter XV

"I need all the friends I can get."
Quasimodo

WHILE MY LIFE may seem convoluted and depressing at times, at least there is one being who never turns from me in my hours of need.

"Gleep!"

I've never understood how a dragon's tongue can be slimy and sandpapery at the same time, but it is. Well, at least the one belonging to *my* dragon is.

"Down, fella...dow...hey! C'mon, Gleep. Stop it!"

"Gleep!" my pet declared as he deftly dodged my hands and left one more slimy trail across my face.

Obedient to a fault. They say you can judge a man's leadership ability by how well he handles animals.

"Darn it, Gleep! This is serious!"

I've often tried to convince Aahz that my dragon actually understands what I say. Whether that was the case here or if he was just sensitive to my tone, Gleep sank back on his haunches and cocked his head attentively.

"That's better," I sighed, daring to breathe through my nose again. Dragons have notoriously bad breath (hence the expression "dragon mouth"), and my pet's displays of affection had the unfortunate side effect of making me feel more than slightly faint. Of course, even breathing through my mouth, I could still taste it.

"You see, I've got a problem...well, several problems, and I thought maybe talking them out without being interrupted might..."

"Gleep!"

The tongue flicked out again, this time catching me with my mouth open. While I love my pet, there are times I wish he were...smaller. Times like this...and when I have to clean out his litter box.

"You want I should lean on the dragon for you, Boss?"

I looked around and discovered Nunzio sitting on one of the garden benches.

"Oh. Hi, Nunzio. What are you doing here? I thought you and Guido usually made yourself scarce when I was exercising Gleep."

"That's usually," the bodyguard shrugged. "My cousin and me, we talked it over and decided with this Ax fella on the loose that one of us should stick with you all the time, know what I mean? Right now it's my shift, and I'll be hangin' tight...no matter what you're doin'."

"I appreciate that, but I don't think there's any danger of getting hit here. I already decided not to take Gleep outside until the coast is clear. No sense tempting fate."

That was at least partially true. What I had really decided was that I didn't want to give the Ax a chance to strike at me through my pet. Aahz already complained enough about having a dragon in residence without adding fuel to the fire. Of course, if my suspicions were correct and Bunny *was* the Ax...

"Better safe than sorry...and you didn't answer my question. You want I should lean on the dragon?"

Sometimes the logic of my bodyguards eluded me completely.

"No. I mean, why should you lean on Gleep? You look comfortable where you are."

Nunzio rolled his eyes. "I don't mean 'lean on him' like really lean on him. I mean, do you want me to bend him a little? You know, rough him up some. I stay outta things between you and your partner, but you shouldn't have to put up with that kind of guff from a dragon."

"He's just being friendly."

"Friendly, schmendly. From what I've seen, you're in more danger from getting knocked off by your own pet than by anyone else I've seen at the Bazaar. All I've ever asked is that you let me do my job....I *am* supposed to be guardin' your body, ya' know. That's how my position got its lofty title."

Not for the first time, I was impressed by Nunzio's total devotion to his work. For a moment I was tempted to let him do what he wanted. At the last minute, though, an image flashed through my mind of my outsized bodyguard and my dragon going at it hammer and tongs in the middle of the garden.

"Umm...thanks, but I think I'll pass, Nunzio. Gleep can be a pain sometimes, but I kind of like him jumping all over me once in a while. It makes me feel loved. Besides, I wouldn't want to see him get hurt...or you either, for that matter."

"Jumpin' up on you is one thing. Doin' it when you don't want him to is sompin' else. Besides, I wouldn't hurt him. I'd just...here, let me show you!"

Before I could stop him, he was on his feet, taking a straddle-legged stance facing my dragon.

"C'mere, Gleep. C'mon, fella."

126

My pet's head snapped around, then he went bounding toward what he thought was a new playmate.

"Nunzio. I..."

Just as the dragon reached him, my bodyguard held out a hand, palm outward.

"Stop, Gleep! Sit! I said SIT!!"

What happened next I had to reconstruct later from replaying my memory, it happened so fast.

Nunzio's hand snaked out and closed over Gleep's snout. With a jerk he pulled the nose down until it was under my pet's head, then pushed up sharply.

In mid-stride the dragon's haunches dropped into a sitting position and he stopped, all the while batting his eyelashes in bewilderment.

"Now stay. Stay!!"

My bodyguard carefully opened his hand and stepped back, holding his palm flat in front of my pet's face.

Gleep quivered slightly but didn't budge from his sitting position.

"See, Boss? He'll mind," Nunzio called over his shoulder. "Ya just gotta be firm with him."

I suddenly realized my jaw was dangling somewhere around my knees. "What...that's incredible, Nunzio! How did you...what did you..."

"I guess you never knew," he grinned. "I used ta be an animal trainer...mostly the nasty ones for shows, know what I mean?"

"An animal trainer?"

"Yeah. It seemed like a logical extension of bein' a schoolteacher...only without the parents to worry about."

I had to sit down. Between the demonstration with Gleep and the sudden insight to his background, Nunzio had my brain on overload.

"An animal trainer *and* a schoolteacher."

"That's right. Say, you want I should work with

127

your dragon some more now that he's quieted down?"

"No. Let him run for a while. This is supposed to be his exercise time."

"You're the Boss."

He turned toward Gleep and clapped his hands sharply. The dragon bounded backwards, then crouched close to the ground, ready to play.

"Get it, boy!"

Moving with surprising believability, the bodyguard scooped an imaginary ball from the ground and pretended to throw it to the far end of the garden.

Gleep spun around and sprinted off in the direction of the "throw," flattening a bench and two shrubs as he went.

"Simply amazing," I murmured.

"I didn't mean to butt in," Nunzio said, sinking into the seat beside me. "It just looked like you wanted to talk and your dragon wanted to frolic."

"It's all right. I'd rather talk to you, anyway."

I was moderately astounded to discover this was true. I'd always been a bit of a loner, but lately it seemed I not only was able to talk to people, I enjoyed it. I hoped it wouldn't seriously change my friendship with Gleep.

"Me? Sure, Boss. What did you want to talk about?"

"Oh, nothing special. I guess I just realized we've never really talked, just the two of us. Tell me, how do you like our operation here?"

"It's okay, I guess. Never really thought about it much. It's not your run-of-the-mill Mob operation, that much is for sure. You got some strange people hangin' around you...but they're nice. I'd give my right arm for any one of them, they're so nice. That's different right there. Most outfits, everybody's tryin' to get ahead...so they spend more time watchin' each other than they do scopin' the opposition. Here, everybody covers for each other instead of nudging the other guy out."

"Do you want to get ahead, Nunzio?"

128

"Yes and no, know what I mean? I don't want to be doin' the same thing the rest of my life, but I'm not pushy to get to the top. Actually, I kinda like workin' for someone else. I let them make the big decisions, then all I gotta do is figure out how to make my part happen."

"You certainly do your part around here," I nodded. "I never knew before how hard a bodyguard works."

"Really? Gee, it's good to hear you say that, Boss. Sometimes Guido and me, we feel like dead weight around here. Maybe that's why we work so hard to do our jobs. I never thought much about whether I do or don't like it here. I mean, I go where I'm assigned and do what I'm told, so it doesn't matter what I think. Right? What I do know, though, is that I'd be real sorry if I had to leave. Nobody's ever treated me like you and your crew do."

Nunzio might not be an intellectual giant or the swiftest wit I've known, but I found his simple honesty touching...not to mention the loyalty it implied.

"Well, you've got a job here as long as I've got anything to say about it." I assured him.

"Thanks, Boss. I was startin' to get a little tired of how the Mob operates, know what I mean?" That rang a bell in my mind.

"Speaking of that, Nunzio, do you think the Mob would ever get involved with something like this character assassination thing?"

The bodyguard's brow furrowed with the effort of thinking.

"Naw!" he said at last. "Mostly people pay us *not* to do things. If we do have to do a number on someone, it's usually to make an example of them and we do something flashy like burn down their house or break their legs. Who would know it if we wrecked their career? What Tananda was sayin' about the Ax was interesting, but it's just not our style."

"Not even for the right price?" I urged. "How much

do you think it would take to get Don Bruce to send someone in here after us?"

"I dunno. I'd have to say at least...wait a minute! Are you askin' if Bunny's the Ax?"

"Well, she did..."

"Forget it, Boss. Even if she could handle the job, which I'm not too sure she could, Don Bruce would never send her after you. Heck, you're one of his favorite chieftains right now. You should hear him..."

Nunzio suddenly pressed his palms against his cheeks to make exaggerated jowls as he spoke. "...Dat Skeeve, he's really got it on the ball, know what I mean? Mercy! If I had a hundred like him I could take over dis whole organization."

His imitation of Don Bruce was so perfect I had to laugh.

"That's great, Nunzio. Has he ever seen you do that?"

"I'm stil employed and breathin', aren't I?" he winked. "Seriously, though. You're barkin' up the wrong tree with Bunny. Believe me, you're the apple of her uncle's eye right now."

"I suppose you're right," I sighed. "If you are, though, it leaves me right back where I started. Who is the Ax and what can..."

"Hi guys! Is that a private conversation, or can anyone join?"

We glanced up to find Bunny and Markie entering the garden.

"C'mon over, Bunny!" I waved, nudging Nunzio slightly in the ribs. "We were just going to..."

"GLEEP!!!"

Suddenly my dragon was in front of me. Crouching and tense, he didn't look playful at all. I had only seen him like this a couple of times before, and then...

"STOP IT, GLEEP! GLEEP!!!" I screamed, realizing too late what was about to happen.

130

Fortunately, Nunzio was quicker than I was. From his sitting position he threw himself forward in a body check against my pet's neck, just as the dragon let loose with a stream of fire. The flames leapt forward to harmlessly scorch a wall.

Bunny swept Markie behind her with one arm.

"Geez! What was..."

"I'll get him!" Markie cried, balling up her fists.

"MARKIE!! STOP!!"

"But Daddy..."

"Just hold it. Okay? Nunzio?"

"I've got him, Boss," he called, both hands wrapped securely around Gleep's snout as the dragon struggled to get free.

"Bunny! You and Markie get inside! Now!!!"

The two of them hurried from sight, and I turned my attention to my pet.

Gleep seemed to have calmed down as fast as he had exploded, now that Bunny and Markie were gone. Nunzio was stroking his neck soothingly while staring at me in wide-eyed amazement.

"I dunno what happened there, Boss, but he seems okay now."

"What happened," I said grimly, "was Gleep trying to protect me from something or someone he saw as a threat."

"But Boss..."

"Look Nunzio, I know you mean well, but Gleep and I go back a long way. I trust his instincts more than I do my own judgment."

"But..."

"I want you to do two things right away. First, put Gleep back in his stable...I think he's had enough exercise for one day. Then get word to Don Bruce. I want to have a little talk with him about his 'present'!"

Chapter XVI

"I thought we were friends!"

Banquo

I TELL YOU, partner, this is crazy!"

"Like heck it is!"

"Bunny can't be the Ax! She's a space cadet."

"That's what she'd like us to think. I found out different!"

"Really? How?"

"By . . . well, by talking to her."

I spotted the flaw in my logic as soon as I said it, and Aahz wasn't far behind.

"Skeeve," he said solemnly, "has it occurred to you that if she's the Ax and you're her target, that you would probably be the last person she would relax around? Do you really think you could trick her into giving away her I.Q. in a simple conversation?"

"Well . . . maybe she was being clever. It could be

that it was her way of trying to throw us off the track."

My partner didn't say anything to that. He just cocked his head and raised one eyebrow *very* high.

"It *could* be," I repeated lamely.

"C'mon, Skeeve. Give."

"What?"

"Even you need more evidence than that before you go off half-cocked. What are you holding back?"

He had me. I was just afraid that he was going to find my real reason even less believable than the one I had already stated.

"Okay," I said with a sigh. "If you really want to know, what finally convinced me was that Gleep doesn't like her."

"Gleep? You mean that stupid dragon of yours? That Gleep?"

"Gleep isn't st . . ."

"Partner, your dragon doesn't like *me!* That doesn't make me the Ax!!"

"He's never tried to fry you, either!"

That one stopped him for a moment. "He did that? He really let fly at Bunny?"

"That's right. If Nunzio hadn't been there . . ."

As if summoned by the mention of his name, the bodyguard stuck his head into the room.

"Hey, Boss! Don Bruce is here."

"Show him in."

"I still think you're making a mistake," Aahz warned, leaning against a wall.

"Maybe," I said grimly. "With luck I'll get Don Bruce to confirm my suspicions before I show my cards."

"This I've got to see."

"There you are, Skeeve. The boys said you wanted to see me."

Don Bruce is the Mob's fairy godfather. I've never seen him dressed in anything that wasn't lavender, and today was no exception. His ensemble included shorts, sandals, a floppy brimmed hat, and a sports shirt with large dark purple flowers printed all over it. Maybe my wardrobe sessions with Bunny were making me overly sensitive on the subject of clothes, but his attire hardly seemed appropriate for one of the most powerful men in the Mob.

Even his dark glasses had violet lenses.

"You know, this is quite a place you got here. Never been here before, but I heard a lot about it in the yearly report. It doesn't look this big from the outside."

"We like to keep a low profile," I said.

"Yeah, I know. It's like I keep tellin' 'em back at Mob Central, you run a class operation. I like that. Makes us all look good."

I was starting to feel a little uncomfortable. The last thing I wanted to discuss with Don Bruce was our current operation.

"Like some wine?" Aahz chimed in, coming to my rescue.

"It's a little early, but why not? So! What is it you wanted to see me about?"

"It's about Bunny."

"Bunny? Oh yeah. How's she workin' out?"

Even if I hadn't already been suspicious, Don Bruce's response would have seemed overly casual. Aahz caught it too, raising his eyebrow again as he poured the wine.

"I thought we should have a little chat about why you sent her here."

"What's to chat about? You needed a moll, and I figured..."

"I mean the *real* reason."

Our guest paused, glanced back and forth between Aahz and me a couple of times, then shrugged his shoulders. "She told you, huh? Funny, I would have thought that was one secret she would have kept."

"Actually, I figured it out all by myself. In fact, when the subject came up, she denied it."

"Always said you were smart, Skeeve. Now I see you're smart enough to get me to admit to what you couldn't trick out of Bunny. Pretty good."

I shot a triumphant glance at Aahz, who was suddenly very busy with the wine. Despite my feeling of victory over having puzzled out the identity of the Ax, I was still more than a little annoyed.

"What I can't figure out," I said, "is why you tried it in the first place. I've always played it pretty straight with you."

At least Don Bruce had the grace to look embarrassed. "I know, I know. It seemed like a good idea at the time, is all. I was in a bit of a spot, and it seemed like a harmless way out."

"Harmless? Harmless! That's my whole life and career we're talking about."

"Hey! C'mon, Skeeve. Aren't you exaggerating a little bit there! I don't think. . . ."

"Exaggerating??"

"Well, I still think you'd make a good husband for her. . ."

"Exaggerating? Aahz, are you listening to. . ."

As I turned to appeal to my partner, I noticed he was laughing so hard he was spilling the wine. Of all the reactions I might have expected from him, laughing wasn't. . .

Then it hit me.

"Husband?!?!?"

"Of course. Isn't that what we've been talkin' about?"

"Skeeve here thinks that your niece is the Ax and that you turned her loose on him to destroy his career," my partner managed between gasps.

"The Ax???"

"HUSBAND????"

"Are you crazy??"

"One of us is!!"

"How about both?" Aahz grinned, stepping between us. "Wine, anyone?"

"But he said..."

"What about..."

"Gentlemen, gentlemen. It's clear that communications have gotten a little fouled up between the two of you. I suggest you each take some wine and we'll start all over again from the top."

Almost mechanically, we both reached for the wine, eyeing each other all the while like angry cats.

"Very good," my partner nodded. "Now then, Don Bruce, as the visiting team I believe you have first serve."

"What's this about the Ax!?!" the mobster demanded, leaning forward so suddenly half the wine sloshed out of his glass.

"You know who the Ax is??"

"I know *what* he is! The question is, what does he have to do with you and Bunny?"

"We've heard recently that someone's hired the Ax to do a number on Skeeve," Aahz supplied.

"...Right about the same time Bunny showed up," I added.

"And that's supposed to make her the Ax?"

"Well, there *has* been some trouble since she arrived."

"Like what?"

"Welll...Tananda left because of things that were said when she found out that Bunny was in my bedroom one morning."

"Tananda? The same Tananda that said 'Hi' to me when I walked in here today?"

"She...ummm...came back."

"I see. What else?"

"She scared off my girlfriend."

"Girlfriend? You got a girlfriend?"

"Well, not exactly...but I might have had one if Bunny wasn't here."

"Uh-huh. Aahz, haven't you ever told him the 'bird in the hand' story?"

"I try, but he isn't big on listening."

I can always count on my partner to rally to my defense in times of crisis.

"What else?"

"Ummm..."

"Tell him!" Aahz smiled.

"Tell me what?"

"My dragon doesn't like her."

"I'm not surprised. She's never gotten along with animals...at least the four-footed kind. I don't see where that makes her the Ax, though."

"It's...it's just that on top of the other evidence..."

My voice trailed off in front of Don Bruce's stony stare.

"You know, Skeeve," he said at last. "As much as I like you, there are times, like now, I wish you was on the other side of the law. If the D.A.s put together a case like you do, we could cut our bribe budget by ninety percent, and our attorney's fees by a hundred percent!"

"But..."

"Now listen close, 'cause I'm only goin' to go over this once. You're the representative for the Mob, and *me,* here at the Bazaar. If you look bad, then we look bad. Got it? What possible sense would it make for us to hire someone to make you, and *us,* look bad?"

On the ropes, I glanced at Aahz for support.

"That was going to be the next question *I* was going to ask, partner."

Terrific.

"Well," Don Bruce announced, standing up. "If that's settled, I guess I can go now."

"Not so fast," my partner smiled, holding up a

137

hand. "There's still the matter of the question that Skeeve asked: if Bunny isn't the Ax, what's she doing here? What was that you were saying about a husband?"

The mobster sank back into his chair and reached for his wine, all the while avoiding my eyes.

"I'm not gettin' any younger," he said. "Some day I'm goin' to retire, and I thought I should maybe start lookin' around for a replacement. It's always nice to have 'em in the family...the real family, I mean, and since I got an unmarried niece...."

"Whoa! Wait a minute," Aahz interrupted. "Are you saying that you're considering Skeeve as your eventual replacement in the Mob?"

"It's a possibility. Why not? Like I said, he runs a class operation and he's smart...at least I used to think so."

"Don Bruce I...I don't know what to say," I said honestly.

"Then don't say nothin'!" he responded grimly. "Whatever's goin' to happen is a long way off. That's why I didn't say anything to you direct. I'm not ready to retire yet."

"Oh." I didn't know whether to feel disappointment or relief.

"About Bunny?" my partner prompted.

The mobster shrugged. "What's to say that hasn't already been said? She's my niece, he's one of my favorite chieftains. I thought it would be a good idea to put 'em close to each other and see if anything happened."

"I...I don't know," I said thoughtfully. "I mean, Bunny's nice enough...especially now that I know she isn't the Ax. I just don't think I'm ready to get married yet."

"Didn't say you were," Don Bruce shrugged. "Don't get me wrong, Skeeve. I'm not tryin' to push you into this. I know it'll take time. Like I said, I just fixed it so you two could meet and see if anything develops...that's all. If it works out, fine. If it doesn't, also fine. I'm not about to try to force things or kid myself that you two will make a pair if you won't. If nothing else, you've got a pretty good accountant while you find out...and from lookin' over your financial figures you could use one."

"Izzat so?"

He had finally tweaked Aahz close to home...or his wallet, which in his case is the same thing.

"What's wrong with our finances? We're doing okay."

"Okay isn't soarin'. You boys got no plan. The way I see it, you've spent so much time livin' hand-to-mouth you've never learned what to do with money except stack it and spend it. Bunny can show you how to make your money work for you."

Aahz rubbed his chin thoughtfully. It was interesting to see my partner caught between pride and greed.

"I dunno," he said at last. "It sounds good, and we'll probably look into it eventually, but we're a little tight right now."

"The way I hear it, you're tight all the time," Don Bruce commented drily.

"No. I mean right now we're *really* tight for finances. We've got a lot of capital tied up in the big game tonight."

"Big game? What big game?"

"Skeeve is going head to head with the Sen-Sen Ante Kid at dragon poker tonight. It's a challenge match."

"That's why I wanted to talk to you about Bunny," I said. "Since I thought she was the Ax, I didn't want her around to cause trouble at the game."

"Why didn't anybody tell me about this game?" Don Bruce demanded. "It wasn't in your report!"

"It's come up since then."

"What are the stakes?"

I looked at Aahz. I had been so busy trying to learn

how dragon poker was played that I had never gotten around to asking about the stakes.

For some reason, my partner suddenly looked uncomfortable.

"Table stakes," he said.

"Table stakes?" I frowned. "What's that?"

I half-expected him to tell me he'd explain later, but instead he addressed the subject with surprising enthusiasm.

"In a table stakes game, each of you starts with a certain amount of money. Then you play until one of you is out of chips, or . . ."

"I know what table stakes are," Don Bruce interrupted. "What I want to know is how much you're playing for."

Aahz hesitated, then shrugged. "A quarter of a million each."

"A QUARTER OF A MILLION???"

I hadn't hit that note since my voice changed.

"Didn't you know?" the mobster scowled.

"We hadn't told him," my partner sighed. "I was afraid that if he knew what the stakes were, he'd clutch. We were just going to give him the stack of chips to play without telling him how much they were worth."

"A quarter of a million?" I repeated, a little hoarser this time.

"See?" Aahz grinned. "You're clutching."

"But, Aahz, do we *have* a quarter of a million to spare?"

My partner's grin faded and he started avoiding my eyes.

"I can answer that one, Skeeve," Don Bruce said. *"No one* has a quarter of a million to spare. Even if you've got it, you don't have it to spare, know what I mean?"

"It's not going to take *all* our money," Aahz said slowly. "The others have chipped in out of their savings, too: Tananda, Chumley, Massha, even Guido and Nunzio. We've all got a piece of the action."

"Us too," the mobster declared. "Put the Mob down for half."

I'm not sure who was more surprised, Aahz or me. But Aahz recovered first.

"That's nice of you, Don Bruce, but you don't understand what's really happening here. Skeeve here is a rank beginner at the game. He had one lucky night, and by the time the rumor mill got through with it, he had drawn a challenge from the Kid. He can't refuse without looking foolish, and with the Ax on the loose we can't afford any bad press we can avoid. That's why we're pooling our money, so Skeeve can go in there and lose gracefully. The actual outcome is preordained. The Kid's going to eat him alive."

". . . And maybe you weren't listening earlier," the mobster shot back. "If Skeeve looks bad, we look bad. The Mob backs its people, especially when it comes to public image. Win or lose, we're in for half, okay?"

"If you say so," Aahz shrugged.

". . . And try to save me a couple seats. I'm gonna want to see my boy in action—firsthand."

"It'll cost!"

"Did I ask? Just . . ."

I wasn't really listening to the conversation any more. I hadn't realized before just how solidly my friends were behind me.

A quarter of a million . . .

Right then something solidified in my mind that had been hovering there for several days now. Whatever the others thought, I was going to try my best to win this game!

Chapter XVII

"Shut up and deal!"

F.D.R.

THERE WAS an aura of expectation over the Bazaar that night as we set out for the Even-Odds. At first I thought I was just seeing things differently because of my anticipation and nervousness. As we walked, however, it became more and more apparent that it was not simply my imagination.

Not a single vendor or shop shill approached us, not a Deveel hailed us with a proposed bargain. On the contrary, as we proceeded along the aisles, conversation and business ground to a halt as everyone turned to watch us pass. A few called out their wishes of "good luck" or friendly gibes about seeing me after the game, but for the most part they simply stared in silent fascination.

If I had ever had any doubts as to the existence or

extent of the rumor mill and grapevine at the Bazaar, that night put them to rest forever. Everybody and I mean *everybody* knew who I was, where I was going, and what was waiting for me.

In some ways it was fun. I've noted earlier that I generally kept a low profile in the immediate neighborhood and have gotten used to walking around unnoticed. My recent shopping trips had gained me a certain notoriety, but it was nothing compared to this. Tonight, I was a full-blown celebrity! Realizing the uncertainty of the game's outcome, I decided to seize the moment and play my part to the hilt.

To a certain degree it was easy. We already made quite a procession. Guido and Nunzio were decked out in their working clothes of trenchcoats and weapons and preceded us, clearing a path through the gawkers. Tananda and Chumley brought up the rear looking positively grim as they eyeballed anyone who seemed to be edging too close. Aahz was walking just ahead of me, carrying our stake money in two large bags. If anyone entertained the thought of intercepting us for the money, all they had to do was look at Aahz's swagger and the gleam in his yellow eyes, and they would suddenly decide there were easier ways to get rich...like wrestling dragons or panning for gold in a swamp.

We had left Markie back at our place over her loud and indignant protests. I had stood firm, though. This game was going to be rough enough without having her around as a distraction. Massha had volunteered to stay with her, claiming she was far too nervous about the game to enjoy watching it anyway.

Bunny was decked out in a clinging outfit in brilliant white and hung on my arm like I was the most important thing in her life. More than a few envious eyes darted from her to me and back again.

No one was kidding anyone, though, as to who the center of attention was. You guessed it. Me! After all, I was the one on my way to lock horns with the legendary Sen-Sen Ante Kid on his own terrain...a card table. Bunny had chosen my clothes for me, and I was resplendent in a dark maroon open-necked shirt with light charcoal gray slacks and vest. I felt and looked like a million...well, make that a quarter of a million. If I was going to have my head handed to me tonight, I was at least going to be able to accept it in style...which was the whole point of this exercise, anyway.

I didn't even try to match Aahz's strut, knowing I would only suffer by comparison. Instead, I contented myself with maintaining a slow, measured, dignified pace as I nodded and waved at the well-wishers. The idea was to exude unhurried confidence. In actuality, it made me feel like I was on the way to the gallows, but I did my best to hide it and keep smiling.

The crowds got progressively thicker as we neared the Even-Odds, and I realized with some astonishment that this was because of the game. Those without the clout or the money to get space inside were loitering around the area in hopes of being one of the first to hear about the game's outcome. I had known that gambling was big at the Bazaar, but I never thought it was *this* popular.

The assemblage melted away before us, clearing a path to the door. I began to recognize faces in the crowd, people I knew. There was Gus waving enthusiastically at me, and over there...

"Vic!"

I veered from our straight line and the whole procession ground to a halt.

"Hi, Skeeve!" the vampire smiled, clapping me on the shoulder. "Good luck tonight!"

"I'm going to need it!" I confided. "Seriously, though, I've been meaning to stop by and thank you for your warning about the Ax."

Vic's face fell. "You might have trouble finding me.

I'm about to lose my office."

"Really? Is business that bad?"

"Worse. There's an awful lot of competition here."

"Well, tell you what. Why don't you stop by my place tomorrow and we'll talk. Maybe we can work out a small loan or maybe even subcontract some assignments until you're established."

"Gee. Thanks, Skeeve!"

A sudden inspiration hit me. "Come by around noon. We'll do lunch!"

It seemed like a really good idea to me. I wondered why businessmen hadn't thought of talking out ideas over lunch before! For some reason, Vic winced before returning my smile.

"Lunch it is," he said.

"Umm...I hate to interrupt, partner, but you *do* have an appointment you're supposed to be at."

"Right, Aahz. Vic! Tomorrow!"

With that, I allowed myself to be ushered into the Even-Odds.

A ripple of applause broke out as I entered the main bar and gaming room, and I barely caught myself from turning to look behind me. For me or against me, the people were here to watch the game and if nothing else were grateful to me for providing the evening's entertainment.

Terrific. I was about to risk a quarter of a million in gold so that folks wouldn't have to watch summer reruns.

The club had been rearranged since the last time I was there. One card table stood alone in the center of the room, while scores of people lined the walls. While the crowd outside might have been larger, the group inside the club made up with clout what they lacked in numbers. While I didn't begin to recognize everyone, the ones I did spot led me to believe that the 'Who's Who' of Deva was assembled to watch the game. Hay-ner, my landlord and leader of the Devan Chamber of Commerce was there along with his usual clutch of cronies. He nodded politely when our eyes met, but I suspected he was really hoping to see me lose.

Don Bruce was there as promised, and raised his hands over his head, clenched them together, and gave them a brief shake, smiling all the while. I guessed it was some sign of encouragement. At the very least, I hoped I wasn't being hailed with some secet Mob death sign. Of course, that didn't occur to me until after I had waved back.

"Skeeve. SKEEVE! Have you got a moment?"

I glanced around to find the Geek standing at my elbow.

"Sure, Geek," I shrugged. "What can I do for you?"

The Deveel seemed extremely nervous, his complexion several shades off its normal hue. "I...you can promise not to hold a grudge. I promise you that tonight was none of my doing. All I did was make the arrangements after the Kid issued the challenge. I didn't give him your name...honest."

To say the least, I found his attitude surprising.

"Sure, Geek. I never thought you..."

"If I had known it would lead to this, I never would have invited you to my game in the first place, much less..."

I was suddenly very alert.

"Wait a minute, Geek! What are you talking about?"

"You're outclassed!" the Deveel explained, glancing around fearfully. "You don't stand a chance against the Kid. I just want you to understand, if you lose all your money tonight, that I didn't mean to set you up. I don't want you or your crew looking for me with blood in your respective eyes."

Now, as you know, I knew that I was outclassed. What intrigued me was that the Geek knew it, too.

146

"Geek, I think we'd better..."

A loud burst of applause and cheers interrupted me. By the time I got through craning my neck to see what was going on, the Geek had disappeared into the crowd. With that discussion closed, I turned my attention again to the subject at hand.

"Who's that?" I said, nodding toward the figure that had just entered the club.

Aahz slid a comforting arm around my shoulders.

"That's him. That's the Sen-Sen Ante Kid."

"THAT'S the Kid???!!"

The man in the door was enormous, he was huge...that is to say, he was Massha's size. For some reason, I had been expecting someone closer to my own age. This character, though, was something else.

He was totally hairless, no beard, no eyebrows, and completely bald. His skin was light blue in color, and that combined with his fat and and wrinkles gave the overall impression of a half-deflated blue bowling ball. His eyes were extremely dark, however, and glittered slightly as they fixed on me.

"That's the Kid?" I repeated.

Aahz shrugged. "He's had the title for a long time."

The man-mountain had two bags with him which looked very similar to the ones Aahz had carried for us. He handed them casually to one of the onlookers.

"Cash me in!" he ordered in a booming voice. "I hear there's a game here tonight."

For some reason, this brought a loud round of laughter and applause from the audience. I didn't think it was all that funny, but I smiled politely. The Kid's eyes noted my lack of enthusiasm and glittered with increased ferocity.

"You must be the Great Skeeve."

His voice was a dangerous purr, but it still reverberated off the walls. He moved toward me with a surprisingly light tread, holding out his hand in welcome.

The crowd seemed to hold its breath.

"...And you must be the one they call the Sen-Sen Ante Kid." I responded, abandoning my hand into his grip.

Again I was surprised...this time by the gentleness of his handshake.

"I just hope your magic isn't as good as your reputation."

"That's funny, I was just hoping your luck is as bad as your jokes."

I didn't mean to be offensive. The words just kind of slipped out before I could stop them.

The Kid's face froze.

I wished someone else would say something to change the subject, but the room echoed with deathly quiet.

Suddenly, my opponent threw his head back and laughed heartily. "I like that!" he declared. "You know, no one else has ever had the nerve to tell me my jokes stink. I'm starting to see where you had the guts to accept my little challenge."

The room came to life, everybody talking or laughing at the same time. I felt like I had just passed some kind of initiation ritual. A wave of relief broke over me...but it was tinged with something else. I found myself liking the Kid. Young or not, he was definitely not the boogey-man I had been expecting.

"Thanks, Kid," I said quietly, taking advantage of the cover noise. "I must admit, I appreciate someone else who can laugh at themselves. I have to do it so often myself."

"Ain't that the truth," he murmured back, glancing around to be sure no one else was listening in. "If you let it, all this stuff can go to your head. Say, would you like a drink or something before we get started?"

"That confident I'm not," I laughed. "I want to have a clear head when we square off."

"Suit yourself," he shrugged.

Before I could say anything else, he turned to the crowd and raised his voice again. "Can you keep it down?" he roared. "We're ready to play cards up here!"

Like magic, the noise stopped and all eyes turned to the two of us again.

I found myself wishing I had accepted the drink.

Chapter XVIII

"Cast your fate to the winds."
L. Bernstein

THE TABLE was waiting for us. There were only two chairs with chips stacked neatly in front of them.

I had a sudden moment of panic when I realized I didn't know which chair was facing south, but Aahz came to my rescue. Darting out of the crowd, he pulled out one chair and held it for me to sit in. To the crowd it looked like a polite gesture, but my friends knew I had come dangerously close to changing the rules I had labored so hard to memorize.

"Cards!" the Kid ordered, holding out one hand as he eased into the chair facing me.

A new deck materialized in his hand. He examined it like a glass of fine wine, holding it up to the light to be sure the wrapping was intact and even sniffing the seal to be sure the factory glue was the same.

Satisfied, he offered the deck to me. I smiled and spread my hands to show I was satisfied. I mean, heck! If he hadn't found anything wrong, it was a cinch that I wouldn't be able to detect any foul play.

The gesture seemed to impress him though, and he gave me a small bow before opening the deck. Once the cards were out of the box, his pudgy fingers seemed to take on a life of their own. Moving swiftly, they removed the jokers and cast them aside, then began peeling cards off the deck two at a time, one from the top and one from the bottom.

Watching the process, I began to realize why his handshake had been so gentle. Large as they were, his fingers were graceful, delicate, and sensitive as they went about their task. These were not the hands of a rough laborer, or even a fighter. They existed to do one thing: to handle a deck of cards.

By now the deck had been rough mixed. The Kid scooped up the pile, squared it, then gave it several quick shuffles. His moves were so precise he didn't even have to re-square the deck when he was done. . .just set it on the center of the table.

"Cut for deal?" he asked.

I repeated my earlier gesture. "Be my guest."

Even this seemed to impress the Kid. . .and the crowd. A low murmur rippled around the room as the pluses and minuses of my move were discussed. The truth of the matter was that after watching the Kid handle the deck, I was embarrassed to show my own lack of skill.

He reached for the deck, and the cards sprang to life again. With a hypnotic rhythm he began cutting the deck and riffing the cards together, all the while staring at me with unblinking eyes. I knew I was being psyched out, but was powerless to fight the effect.

"For the ante, shall we say one thousand?"

"Let's say five thousand." I returned.

152

The rhythm faltered. The Kid realized he had slipped and moved swiftly to cover it. Setting the cards aside for a moment, he reached for his chips.

"Five thousand it is," he said, tossing a handful into the center of the table. "And...my trademark."

A small white breath mint followed the chips into the pot.

I was counting out my own chips when something occurred to me.

"How much is that worth?" I said, pointing at the mint.

That surprised my opponent.

"What? The mint? One copper a roll. But you don't have to..."

Before he had finished speaking I added a small coin to my chips, pushed them into the center of the table, grabbed his mint, and popped it into my mouth.

This time the audience actually gasped before lapsing into silence. For several heartbeats there was no sound in the room except the mint crunching between my teeth. I almost regretted my bold move. The mint was incredibly strong.

Finally the Kid grinned.

"I see. You eat my luck, eh? Good. Very good. You'll find, though, that it takes more than that to disturb my game."

His tone was jovial, but his eyes darkened even more than they had been and his shuffling took on a sharper, more vengeful tone. I knew I had scored a hit.

I stole a glance at Aahz, who winked at me broadly. "Cut!"

The deck was in front of me. Moving with forced nonchalance, I cut the deck roughly in half, then leaned back in my chair. While I tried to appear casual, inside I was crossing my fingers and toes and everything else crossable. I had devised my strategy on my own and hadn't discussed it with anyone...not even Aahz. Now we got to see how it worked.

One card...two cards...three cards came gliding across the table to me, face down. They slid to a stop neatly aligned, another tribute to the Kid's skill, and lay there like land mines.

I ignored them, waiting for the next card.

It came, coasting to a stop face up next to its brethren. It was the seven of diamonds and the Kid dealt himself...

The ten of diamonds. A ten!

The rules came back to me like a song I didn't want to remember. A ten face up meant my seven was dead...valueless.

"So much for eating my luck, eh?" the Kid chuckled, taking a quick glance at his hole cards. "My ten will go...five thousand."

"...And up five."

The gasp from the crowd was louder this time... possibly because my coaches had joined in. I heard Aahz clear his throat noisily, but wouldn't look in his direction. The Kid was staring at me in undisguised surprise. Apparently he had either expected me to fold or call...possibly because that would have been the sane thing to do.

"You're awfully proud of that dead card," he said thoughtfully. "All right. I'll call. Pot's right."

Two more cards floated onto the table face up. I got a ten! The ten of clubs, to be specific. That canceled his ten and made my seven live again.

The Kid got the unicorn of hearts. Wild card! Now I had ten-seven high against his pair of tens showing.

Terrific.

"I won't try to kid you." my opponent smiled. "A pair of tens is worth...twenty thousand."

"...And up twenty."

The Kid's smile faded. His eyes flicked quickly to my cards, then he nodded. "Call."

154

No comment. No witty banter. I had him thinking.

The next cards were en route. The three of hearts slid into my lineup. A dead card. Opposing it, the Kid got...

The ten of hearts!

I was now looking at three tens against my ten-seven high! For a moment my resolve wavered, but I shored it up again. I was in too far to change now.

The Kid was eyeing me thoughtfully. "I don't supose you'd go thirty on that?" he said.

"I'll not only go it, I'll raise you thirty."

There were muffled exclamations of disbelief in the room...and some not so muffled. I recognized the voices of some of the latter.

The Kid just shook his head and pushed the appropriate number of chips into the pot without a word. The crowd lapsed into silence and craned their necks to see the next cards.

The dragon of spades to me, and the ogre of hearts to the Kid.

No apparent help for either hand...except that now the Kid had three hearts face up.

We both studied each other's cards for a few moments.

"I'll admit I can't figure out what you're betting, Skeeve," my opponent sighed. "But this hand's worth fifty."

"...And up fifty."

Instead of responding, the Kid leaned back in his chair and stared at me.

"Check me on this," he said. "Either I've missed it completely, or you haven't looked at your hole cards yet."

"That's right."

The crowd started muttering again. At least some of them had missed that point.

"So you're betting blind?"

"Right."

"...And raising into me to boot."

I nodded.

"I don't get it. How do you expect to win?"

I regarded him for a moment before I answered. To say the least, I had the room's undivided attention.

"Kid, you're the best there is at dragon poker. You've spent years honing your skills to be the best, and nothing that happens here tonight is going to change that. Me, I'm lucky...if you can call it that. I got lucky one night, and that somehow earned me the chance to play this game with you tonight. That's why I'm betting the way I am."

The Kid shook his head. "Maybe I'm slow, but I still don't get it."

"In the long run, your skill would beat my luck. It always does. I figure the only chance I've got is to juice the betting on this one hand...go for broke. All the skill in the dimensions can't change the outcome of one hand. That's luck...which puts us on an equal footing."

My opponent digested this for a few moments, then threw back his head and gave a bark of laughter.

"I love it!" he crowed. "A half million pot riding on one hand. Skeeve, I like your style. Win or lose, it's been a pleasure matching wits with you."

"Thank you, Kid. I feel the same way."

"In the meantime, there's this hand to play. I hate to keep all these people hanging in suspense when we already know how the betting's going to go."

He swept the rest of his chips into the pot. "I'll call your raise and raise you back...thirty-five. That's the whole stake."

"Agreed," I said, pushing my chips out.

"Now let's see what we got," he winked, reaching for the deck.

The two of diamonds to me...the eight of clubs to the Kid...then one more card each face down.

The crowd pressed forward as my opponent peered at his last card.

"Skeeve," he said almost regretfully. "You had an interesting strategy there, but my hand's good... real good."

He flipped two of his down cards over.

"Full Dragon...four Ogres and a pair of tens."

"Nice hand." I acknowledged.

"Yeah. Right. Now let's see what you've got."

With as much poise as I could muster, I turned over my hole cards.

Chapter XIX

"Can't you take a joke?"
                    T. Eulenspiegel

MASSHA LOOKED UP from her book and bon-bons as we trooped through the door.

"That was quick," she said. "How did it go?"

"Hi, Massha. Where's Markie?"

"Upstairs in her room. After the second time she tried to sneak out, I sent her to bed and took up sentry duty here by the door. What happened at the game?"

"Well, I still say you were wrong," Aahz growled. "Of all the dumb stunts you've pulled..."

"C'mon, partner. What's done is done. Okay? You're just mad because I didn't check with you first."

"That's the least of..."

"WILL SOMEBODY TELL ME WHAT HAPPENED?"

"What? Oh. Sorry, Massha. I won. Aahz here is

upset because..."

I was suddenly swept up in a gargantuan hug and kiss as my apprentice expressed her delight at the news.

"I'll say he won. In one hand he won," Tananda grinned. "Never seen anything like it."

"Three unicorns and the six of clubs in the hole," Aahz raged. "Three wild cards, which, when used with the once-a-night suit shift rule on the seven of diamonds, yields..."

"A straight-bloody-flush!" Chumley sang. "Which took the Kid's Full Dragon and the largest pot that's ever been seen at the Bazaar."

"I knew you could do it, Daddy!" Markie shrieked, emerging from her hiding spot on the stairs.

So much for sending her to bed early.

"I wish you could have seen the Kid's face, Massha," the troll continued merrily. "I'll bet he wishes now that he carries antacids instead of breath mints."

"You should have seen the crowd. They're going to be talking about this one for years!"

Massha finally let me down and held up a hand.

"Hold it! Wait a minute! I get the feeling I've missed a lap here somewhere. Hot Stuff here won. Right? As in walked away with all the marbles?"

The brother and sister team nodded vigorously. I just tried to get my breath back.

"So how come Green and Scaly is breathing smoke? I should think he'd be leading the cheering."

"BECAUSE HE GAVE THE MONEY AWAY! THAT'S WHY!!!"

"Yes. That would explain it." Massha nodded thoughtfully.

"C'mon, Aahz! I didn't *give* it away."

As I've discovered before, it's a lot easier to find your breath when you're under attack.

"Whoa! Wait!" my apprentice said, stepping between us. "Before you two get started again, talk to Massha.

159

Remember, I'm the one who wasn't there."

"Well, the Kid and I got to talking after the game. He's really a nice guy, and I found out that he had pretty much been betting everything he had . . . "

"That's what he *claimed,*" Aahz snorted. "I think he was making a play for our sympathies."

" . . . and I got to thinking. I had worked hard to be sure that both the Kid's and my reputations would be intact, no matter how the game came out. What I really wanted to do was to retire from the dragon poker circuit and let *him* take on all the hotshot challengers . . . "

"That much I'll agree with."

"Aahz! Just let him tell it. Okay?"

" . . . But he couldn't keep playing if he was broke, which would leave me as the logical target for the up-and-comings, so I let him keep the quarter of a million he had lost . . . "

"See! SEE!!! What did I tell you?"

" . . . as a LOAN so he could use it as a stake in future games . . . . "

"That's when I knew he had . . . a loan??"

I grinned at my partner.

"Uh-huh. As in 'put your money to work for you instead of stacking it,' a concept I believe you found very interesting when it was first broached. Of course, you had already gone off half-cocked and stomped away before we got to that part."

Any sarcasm I had managed to load into my voice was lost on Aahz, which is not surprising when you realize we were talking about money.

"A loan, eh?" he said thoughtfully. "What were the terms?"

"Tell him, Bunny."

"BUNNY??"

"Hey! You weren't there, remember? I decided to see what our accountant could do. Bunny?"

"Well, I've never dealt with stake money before, no

160

pun intended, so I had to kind of feel my way along. I think I got us a pretty good arrangement, though."

"Which was..."

"Until the Kid pays us back... and it's got to be paid back in full, no partial payments, we get half his winnings."

"Hmmm," my partner murmured. "Not bad."

"If you can think of anything else I should have asked for, I'm open to..."

"If he could think of anything else," I said, winking at her, "you can believe he would have roared it out by now. You did great, Bunny."

"Gee. Thanks, Skeeve."

"Now then, if someone would be so kind as to break out the wine, I feel like celebrating."

"Of course, Boss, you realize that now a lot of people know that you've got a lot of cash on hand," Guido pointed out, edging close to me. "As soon as Nunzio gets back, I think we'd better take a look at beefin' up security on the place, know what I mean?"

"Where is Nunzio, anyway?" Massha said, peering around.

"He'll be along in a bit," I smiled. "I had a little errand for him after the game."

"Well, here's to you, Skeeve!" Chumley called, lifting his goblet aloft. "After all our worrying about whether your reputation could survive a match with the Kid, I dare say you came out of it well ahead of where you were before."

"That's right," his sister giggled. "I wonder what the Ax thinks about what happened."

That was the cue I had been waiting for. I took a deep breath and a deeper drink of wine, then assumed my most casual manner.

"Why bother speculating, Tananda? Why not ask direct?"

"What's that, Skeeve?"

"I said, why not ask the Ax directly? After all, she's in the room right now."

The gaiety of the mood vanished in an eyeblink as everybody stared at me.

"Partner," Aahz murmured, "I thought we settled this when we talked to Don Bruce."

I cut him off with the wave of a hand.

"As a matter of fact, I'm a little curious about what the Ax is thinking myself. Why don't you tell us... Markie?"

My young ward squirmed under the room's combined gaze.

"But, Daddy...I don't...you...oh, heck! You figured it out, huh?"

"Uh-huh." I nodded, not feeling at all triumphant.

She heaved a great sigh. "Oh, well. I was about to throw in the towel anyway. I had just hoped I could beat a retreat before my cover was blown. If you don't mind, I'd like to join you in some of that wine now."

"Help yourself."

"MARKIE?!?"

Aahz had finally recovered enough to make noise. Of course, it comes reflexively to him. The others were still working on it.

"Don't let the little-girl looks fool you, Aahz," she winked. "Folks are small and soft on my dimension. In the right clothes, it's easy to pass yourself off as being younger than you really are...lots younger."

"But...but..."

"Think about it for a minute, Aahz," I said. "You had all the pieces the first day. Kids, particularly little girls, are embarrassing at best, trouble at worst. The trick is that you *expect* them to be trouble, so you don't even consider the possibility that what they're doing could be premeditated and planned."

I paused to take a sip of wine, and for once no one interrupted me with questions.

"If you look back on it, most of the problems we've been having have originated directly or indirectly from Markie. She mouthed off about Bunny being in my bed to get Tananda upset, and when that didn't work she made a few digs about her living here free that got her thinking about leaving...just like she deliberately made Massha look bad in the middle of her magic lesson for the same reason, to get her to leave."

"Almost worked, too," my apprentice observed thoughtfully.

"The business in the Bazaar was no accident, either," I continued. "All she had to do was wait for the right opportunity to pretend to get mad so we wouldn't suspect she was blasting things deliberately. If you recall, she even tried to convince me that I didn't need to take dragon poker lessons."

"Of course," Markie put in, "that's not easy to do when people think you're a kid."

"The biggest clue was Gleep. I thought he was trying to protect me from Bunny, but it was Markie he was really after. I keep telling you that he's smarter than you think."

"Remind me to apologize to your dragon," Aahz said, still staring at Markie.

"It was a good plan," she sighed. "Ninety-nine percent of the time it would have worked. The problem was that everyone underestimated you, Skeeve...you and your friends. I didn't think you'd have enough money to pay off the irate merchants after I did a number on their displays, and your friends..."

She shook her head slowly.

"Usually if word gets out that I'm on assignment, it makes my work easier. The target's associates bail out to keep from getting hit in the crossfire, and trying to get them to stay or come back only makes things worse. Part of sinking someone's career is cutting them off from their support network."

She raised her wine in a mock toast to me.

"Your friends wouldn't run...or if they did, they wouldn't stay gone once they heard you were in trouble. That's when I started to have second thoughts about this assignment. I mean, there are some careers that shouldn't be scuttled, and I think yours is one of them. You can take that as a compliment...it's meant as one. That's why I was about to call it quits anyway. I realized my heart just wasn't in my work this time around."

She set down her wine and stood up.

"Well, I guess that's that. I'll go upstairs and pack now. Make you a deal. If you all promise not to tell anyone who the famous Ax is, I'll spread the word that you're so invincible that even the Ax couldn't trip you up. Okay?"

Watching her leave the room, I realized with some surprise that I would miss her. Despite what Aahz had said, it had been kind of nice having a kid around the place.

"That's it?" my partner frowned. "You're just going to let her walk?"

"I was the target. I figure it was my call. Besides, she didn't do any real damage. As Chumley pointed out a second ago, we're further ahead than we were when she arrived."

"Of course, there's the matter of the damages we had to pay for her little magic display at the Bazaar."

For once, I was ahead of my partner when it came to money.

"I haven't forgotten that, Aahz. I just figure to recoup the loss from another source. You see, what finally tipped me off was...wait. Here they are now."

Nunzio was just coming into the room, dragging the Geek with him.

"Hello, Skeeve," the Deveel said, squirming in my bodyguard's grasp. "Your...ah, associate here says you wanted to see me?"

"He tried to sneak out after I told him, Boss," Nunzio squeaked. "That's what took me so long."

"Hello, Geek," I purred. "Have a seat. I want to have a little chat with you about a card game."

"C'mon, Skeeve. I already told you..."

"Sit!"

The Geek dropped into the indicated chair like gravity had suddenly trebled. I had borrowed the tone of voice from Nunzio's dragon-training demonstration. It worked.

"What the Geek was starting to say," I explained, turning to Aahz, "is that before the game tonight he warned me that I was overmatched and asked me not to have any hard feelings...that the game with the Kid wasn't his idea."

"That's right," the Deveel interjected. "Word just got out and..."

"What I'm curious about, however, is how he knew I was outclassed."

I smiled at the Geek, trying to show my teeth the way Aahz does. "You see, I don't want to talk about tonight's game. I was hoping you could give us a little more information about the *other* game...you know, the one where I won Markie?"

The Deveel glanced nervously around the group of assembled scowls.

"I...I don't know what you mean."

"Let me make it easy for you. At this point I figure the game had to be rigged. That's the only way you would know in advance what a weak dragon poker player I am. Somehow you were throwing hands my way to be sure I won big, big enough to include Markie. I'm just curious how you did it without triggering the magic or telepathy monitors."

The Geek seemed to shrink a little in his chair. When he spoke, his voice was so low we could barely hear him.

"Marked cards," he said.

The room exploded.

"MARKED CARDS??"

"But how..."

"Wouldn't that..."

I waved them back to silence.

"It makes sense. Think about it," I instructed. "Specifically, think back to our trip to Limbo. Remember how hard it was to disguise ourselves without using magic? Everybody at the Bazaar gets so used to things being done magically, they forget there are non-magical ways to do the same things..like false beards, or marked cards."

The Geek was on his feet now.

"You can't hold that against me! So someone else paid me to throw the game your way. Heck, I should think you'd be happy. You came out ahead, didn't you? What's to be mad about?"

"I'll bet if I try real hard I could think of something."

"Look, if it's revenge you want, you already got it. I lost a bundle tonight betting against you. You want blood, I'm bleeding!"

The Deveel was sweating visibly now. Then again, he's always been a little nervous around me for some reason.

"Relax, Geek. I'm not going to hurt you. If anything, I'm going to help you...just like you helped me."

"Yeah?" he said suspiciously.

"You say you're short of cash, we'll fix it."

"What!!??" Aahz roared, but Tananda poked him in the ribs and he subsided into sullen silence.

"Bunny?"

"Yeah, Skeeve?"

"First thing tomorrow I want you to run over to the Even-Odds. Go over the books, take inventory, and come up with a fair price for the place."

The Geek blinked.

"My club? But I . . ."

". . . Then draw up an agreement for us to take it off the Geek's hands . . . at half the price you arrive at."

"WHAT!!??" the Deveel screeched, forgetting his fear. "Why should I sell my club for . . ."

". . . More than it will be worth if the word gets out that you're running rigged games?" I finished for him. "Because you're a shrewd businessman, Geek. Besides, you need the money. Right?"

The Geek swallowed hard, then licked his lips before he spoke. "Right."

"How was that, Geek?" Aahz frowned. "I didn't quite hear you."

"I did," I said firmly. "Well, we won't keep you any longer, Geek. I know you'll want to get back to your club and clean up a bit. Otherwise we'll have to reduce the amount of our appraisal."

The Deveel started to snarl something, then thought better of it and slunk out into the night.

"Do you think that will make up for what we had to pay in damages, partner?" I said innocently.

"Skeeve, sometimes you amaze me," Aahz said, lifting his wine in a salute. "Now if there are no more surprises, I'm ready to party."

It was tempting, but I was on a roll and didn't want to let the moment slip away.

"There *is* one more thing," I announced. "Now that we've taken care of the Ax and the Kid, I think we should address the major problem that's come up . . . while everyone is here."

"Major problem?" my partner scowled. "What's that?"

Taking a deep breath, I went for it.

Chapter XX

"So what else is new?"
W. Cronkite

THE WHOLE CREW was staring at me as I rolled my goblet of wine back and forth in my hand, trying to decide where to start.

"If I've seemed a little distracted during this latest crisis," I said at last, "it's because I've been wrestling with another problem that's come to my attention...a big one. So big that, in my mind, the other stuff took a lower priority."

"Whatever you're talking about, partner," Aahz frowned, "I've missed it."

"You just said it, Aahz. The magic word is 'partner.' Things have been going real well for you and me, but we aren't the only ones in this household. When we were talking to Chumley and he said that his life wasn't all beer and skittles, it took me a while to puzzle out what he was talking about, but it finally came clear."

I looked at the troll.

"Business is off for you, isn't it, Chumley?"

"Well, I don't like to complain…"

"I know, but maybe you should once in a while. I had never stopped to think about it before, but you've been getting fewer and fewer assignments since you moved in with us, haven't you?"

"Is that true, Chumley?" Aahz said. "I never noticed…"

"No one's noticed because the attention has always been on us, Aahz. The Aahz and Skeeve team has been taking priority over everything and everyone else. We've been so busy living up to our big-name image that we've missed what it's doing to our colleagues, the ones who have to a large extent been responsible for our success."

"Oh, come now, Skeeve old boy," Chumley laughed uneasily. "I think you're exaggerating a bit there."

"Am I? Your business is off, and so is Tananda's. I hate to say it, but she was right when she left, we are stifling her with our current setup. Guido and Nunzio knock themselves out trying to be super-bodyguards because they're afraid we'll decide we don't really need them and send them packing. Even Massha thinks of herself as a non-contributing team member. Bunny's our newest arrival, and she tried to tell me that the only way she could help us is as an ornament!"

"I feel better about that after tonight, Skeeve," Bunny corrected. "Between negotiating with the Kid and getting the assignment to price out the Even-Odds, I think I can do something for you besides breathe heavy."

"Exactly!" I nodded. "That's what's giving me the courage to propose the plan I've cooked up."

"Plan? What plan?"

"That's what I wanted to talk to you about, Aahz. Actually, what I wanted to talk to all of you about. What we're dealing with in this household isn't really a

169

partnership...it's a company. Everybody in this room contributes to the success of our group as a whole, and I think it's about time we restructured our setup to reflect that. What we really need is a system where all of us have a say as to what's going on. Then clients will be able to approach us as a group, and we quote prices, hand out assignments or subcontract, and share the profits as a group. That's my proposal, for what it's worth. What do the rest of you think?"

The silence stretched on until I started to wonder if they were trying to think of a tactful way to tell me I belonged in a rubber room.

"I don't know, Skeeve," Aahz said at last.

"What aren't you sure of?" I urged.

"I don't know if we should call ourselves Magic, Inc., or Chaos, Ltd."

"Magic, Inc., has already been used," Tananda argued. "Besides, I think the name should be a little more dignified and formal."

"You do that, then the clients are goin' to be surprised when they actually see us, know what I mean?" Guido put in. "We ain't exactly dignified and formal ourselves."

I leaned back in my chair and took a deep breath. If that was their only concern, my idea was at least deemed worthy of consideration.

Massha caught my eye and winked.

I toasted her back, feeling justifiably smug.

"Does this company accept new applicants?"

We all turned to find Markie in the door, suitcase in her hand.

"I don't think I have to tell you all about my qualifications," she continued, "but I admire this group and would be proud to be a part of it."

The crew exchanged glances.

"Well, Markie..."

"It's still nebulous..."

"You've got the Elemental stuff down cold..."

"What do you think, Skeeve?" Aahz said. "You're the one who's usually big on recruiting old enemies."

"No," I said firmly.

They were all looking at me again.

"Sorry to sound so overbearing right after claiming I wanted everybody to have a say in things," I continued, "but if Markie's in, I'm out."

"What's the problem, Skeeve?" Markie frowned. "I thought we were still on pretty good terms."

"We are," I nodded. "I'm not mad at you. I won't work against your career or hit you or hold a grudge. You were just doing your job."

I raised my head and our eyes met.

"I just can't go along with how you work, is all. You say you admire our group—well, the glue that holds us together is trust. The way you operate is to get people to trust you, then betray it. Even if you stayed loyal to our group, I don't think I want to be associated in business with someone who thinks that's the way to turn a profit."

I stopped there, and no one else raised a voice to contradict me.

Markie picked up her suitcase and started for the door. At the last moment, though, she turned back to me and I could see tears in her eyes.

"I can't argue with what you're saying, Skeeve," she said, "but I can't help wishing you had settled for hitting me and let me join."

There was total silence as she made her departure.

"The young lady has raised a valid point," Chumley said at last. "What is our position on new members?"

"If we're open, I'd like to put Vic's name up for consideration," Massha chimed in.

"First we've got to decide if we need anyone else," Tananda corrected.

"That raises the whole question of free-lance vs.

171

exclusive contracts," Nunzio said. "I don't think that it's realistic to have all our shares equal."

"I've been doodling up a plan on just that point, Nunzio," Bunny called, waving the napkin she had been scribbling on. "If you can hold on for a few minutes, I'll have something to propose officially."

As interested as I was in the proceedings, I had trouble concentrating on what was being said. For some reason, Markie's face kept crowding into my mind.

Sure, what I said was rough, but it was necessary. If you're going to run a business or a team, you've got to set a standard and adhere to it. There's no room for sentimentality. I had done the right thing, hadn't I? Hadn't I?

END